CHRISTMAS EVE DELIVERY

BY
CONNIE COX

First published in Great Britain 2013
by Mills & Boon, an imprint of Harlequin (UK) Limited.
Harlequin (UK) Limited, Eton House,
18-24 Paradise Road, Richmond, Surrey TW9 1SR

© Connie Cox 2013

ISBN: 978 0 263 89924 5

Harlequin (UK) policy is to use papers that are natural, renewable and recyclable products and made from wood grown in sustainable forests. The logging and manufacturing process conform to the legal environmental regulations of the country of origin.

Printed and bound in Spain
by Blackprint CPI, Barcelona

Connie Cox has loved Harlequin Mills & Boon® romances since she was a young teen. To be a Harlequin Mills & Boon® author now is a fantasy come to life. By training, Connie is an electrical engineer. Through her first job, working on nuclear scanners and other medical equipment, she had a unique perspective on the medical world. She is fascinated by the inner strength of medical professionals, who must balance emotional compassion with stoic logic, and is honoured to showcase the passion of these dedicated professionals through her own passion of writing. Married to the boy-next-door, Connie is the proud mother of one terrific daughter and son-in-law and one precocious dachshund.

Connie would love to hear from you. Visit her website at www.ConnieCox.com

Recent titles by Connie Cox:

WHEN THE CAMERAS STOP ROLLING…
HIS HIDDEN AMERICAN BEAUTY
THE BABY WHO SAVED DR CYNICAL
RETURN OF THE REBEL SURGEON

This one's for you, Deseré Steenberg!
Here's to strong men and the brave women who love them!

**Praise for
Connie Cox:**

'Return of the Rebel Surgeon is an emotionally packed
reunion story… I would definitely recommend
reading [it].'
—*HarlequinJunkie* on
RETURN OF THE REBEL SURGEON

**Available in eBook format
from www.millsandboon.co.uk**

CHAPTER ONE

DESERÉ WEDGED HER car into a parking place between a dual-axel diesel truck and a huge silver horse trailer as red dust swirled around her. East Texas dust.

So different from New Orleans pavement.

She put her hand over her stomach. New town. New life. "Here's to us, baby James. To our future." She hefted the bottle of milk she'd purchased at her last gas and restroom stop, toasted her sister's unborn baby and chugged.

Reinforced by lukewarm milk, she gathered her purse along with her courage and opened the door.

The sultriness of the heavy, humid air hit her hard. One step behind was the scent of pine trees and the odor of horse manure.

The pine trees had towered over her as she'd travelled down the unpaved road leading to the rodeo arena. In the dusk, those tall skinny evergreens appeared imposing, like sentinels warning her that she wasn't in the big city anymore.

For the baby's sake, she wouldn't let this alien landscape intimidate her.

"Everything will be just fine." She said it out loud to force conviction.

A gaunt, stooped cowboy with a weathered straw

hat shadowing his leathered face stopped on the way to his truck.

She knew he drove a truck even though she didn't know which one. She knew it had to be a truck because she had the only car in the parking lot.

He put two fingers to the brim of his hat and nodded before asking, "You okay, ma'am?"

"I'm fine. Thank you."

The old man gave her a strong look, half-wary that she might be crazy talking to herself and the other half suspicious of the overdressed stranger in their midst.

She tried to reassure him with the brightest smile she could muster after eight hours of driving with all her worldly goods crammed into her little compact car.

"I'm fine, really."

He glanced at her stomach as if he knew. How could he? She was only four and a half months and had barely begun to show.

She was being fanciful. A fleeting look of no consequence was all it had been.

Working hard to shrug off her supposition, she blamed it on her sensitivity to the situation. On hormones. On paranoia from lack of sleep.

He couldn't know her secret.

Because if he did, the man she had driven all these hundreds of miles to find would know, too. And then where would she be?

She couldn't even think about a near future that bleak.

He had to say yes. There was no other option.

She'd called in the only favor she had and it had been a weak one. A doctor she'd once dated. A relationship that hadn't worked out. What were the odds of that wildcard making the difference?

The odds were already stacked against her and her chances plummeted if the cowboy she was looking for realized she was pregnant.

In her open-toed sandals, she picked her way across the ruts cut into the dried mud and scarce grass sprigs that made up the entrance in front of the arena. Dusky shadows made the short distance seem treacherous.

Ringed by a tall wooden fence, the arena was hidden from her. Looking up, she could see only the glare of the tall lights and the wash of bodies in the stands. Cowboy hats on everyone's heads made each person's features indistinguishable from each other.

How would she ever find him?

With only nineteen dollars and twenty-nine cents in her wallet, she had to find him. She could sleep in her car again, but she needed a few gallons in her gas tank to keep her car rolling and a decent meal to keep the baby healthy.

Her stomach chose that moment to growl. Except for her daily dose of midmorning nausea, her pregnancy kept her continually hungry.

She circled the arena, looking for an opening into this world of rodeo that personified testosterone, muscle and mastery of will.

Carefully, she skirted the hitching posts where horses were tethered with only thin strips of rope or single leather reins. Didn't these monsters know they could pull away with only a shake of their heads?

How far could they kick? A protective hand over her stomach, she gave them wide berth.

Pulling out her thin wallet, she prepared to pay admission, whatever it cost. She had no other choice.

"Excuse me?" She stopped a young girl in perfect make-up, painted-on jeans, embossed boots, long blonde curls and rhinestones in the band of her white cowgirl hat.

"Yes, ma'am?"

Another "ma'am." This time it made her feel more old than honored.

Giving the girl the last smile she had in her, De-seré asked, "Where's the entrance and how much is the entry fee?"

The girl gave a kind, sympathetic glance at her inappropriate tailored slacks, silk blouse and strappy sandals before she waved toward the end of the wooden fence. "All the events are free to watch. Just go right on in. But watch your step, okay?"

Deseré looked down to where the girl pointed. She'd missed a huge pile of horse droppings by scant millimeters.

"Thanks."

As she minced her way toward the stands, she had to get a bit too close for comfort to the massive horses that were either tied to the backs of the stands or were being ridden in various directions from the barns to the arena.

No one else seemed concerned as the tons of muscle on delicate hoofs pranced by so close.

So this was Friday night in Piney Woods, Texas.

"We're definitely not in New Orleans anymore," she whispered to the baby nestled in her womb.

As she approached the full stands, several rows of observers started scooting over, packing themselves in tighter as they made room for her.

One of the cowboys on the end stood. He gave her an appreciative, if curious once-over as he touched the brim of his hat. "Please, ma'am, have my seat. I'll stand."

"Thank you." Instead of sliding onto the hard wooden

bench, Deseré took a deep breath. No turning back from here. "I'm looking for Dr. Hart."

"Jordan will be first one out of the gate as soon as we get started again." He drew his brows together in concern. "You're not needing him, are you? Do I need to go and fetch him for you?"

It was more the other way around. She was hoping—counting on—Dr. Hart needing her. If he didn't, she didn't know what she would do.

Almost on instinct, her hand moved to cover her abdomen. At the last moment she diverted it to the strap of the purse slung across her body.

"No emergency."

"After his ride, I'll tell him you're waiting for him." He waved her toward his vacated seat on the bench. "Best seat in the house."

"Thanks."

"Rusty." He touched his hat again. "Folks call me Rusty."

He left the introduction hanging with his expectant look. What would it hurt to introduce herself?

"Deseré."

"Nice to meet you, Miss Deseré."

Miss Deseré. She knew, even if she'd been wearing a wedding ring that was bigger than Dallas, Rusty would have called her "Miss" as a sign of respect. Among the gentlemen she knew in New Orleans, it was a sign of respect there, too.

The familiar custom eased the tension across her shoulders by the slightest of muscle twitches.

Before she could return the nicety a loudspeaker boomed, "Up next is Jordan Hart, points leader for this event."

Distantly, she heard a deep voice call out, "Cowboy up."

She looked in that direction, to see a calf burst from a narrow chute into the arena. Hot on its heels was a cowboy on a very large red horse.

With only the slightest flick of his wrist, Dr. Jordan Hart unfurled his rope. The stiff loop shot out and fell neatly over the neck of the running calf.

His horse stopped short, jerking the calf to a standstill.

Quicker than she could comprehend, Jordan slid out of his saddle and began taking big strides toward the snared calf as his horse backed away without direction to keep the rope taut, with its end looped around the saddle horn.

He grabbed the calf, tipped it onto its side and wrapped three of its four legs using the short ropes he'd carried in his mouth.

Once done, he threw his hands in the air. Another man looking official with his stopwatch and mounted on a horse that stood as still as a statue called, "Time," as he nodded to someone in the speaker's booth next to the complex structure Rusty had called "*the gate*."

A smattering of applause broke out from the stands. Deseré couldn't help but notice that most of the cheering came from the women and girls, all dressed similarly to the first girl Deseré had met.

If those were his type of women, then she definitely didn't fit his mold.

Not that she needed to be Jordan Hart's type.

She just needed his money.

As Jordan loosened the cinch on his mare, he saw his cousin and ranch foreman, Rusty, approach him.

"Nice run, cuz." Rusty gave Jordan's mare a rub on her neck. She leaned into it, clearly enjoying his touch.

"Thanks."

"Jordan…" Rusty hesitated. "Are you expecting to meet a woman here tonight?"

He quirked his eyebrow at his cousin's cautious question. "No, I'm not."

"Well, there's one waiting for you on the bleachers."

She wouldn't be the first buckle bunny to approach him. Under the brim of his hat, he checked her out.

In her city clothes, she certainly wasn't dressed for a rodeo pickup. He couldn't be sure as she was slumped on the bench, arms tightly wrapped around her huge purse, but he thought she might be five feet seven or so to his six one. Tall enough to kiss without getting a crick in his neck.

Where had that thought come from?

And the accompanying spark in his veins?

At first he was jolted by it. But by his second heartbeat he welcomed it. It had been so long since he'd felt even a flicker of interest.

Gently blowing on that internal ember, he continued to examine her.

Her mink-brown hair shimmered in the bright overhead lights as it fell to her shoulder blades. It was the perfect length. A man could tangle his hands in that silky softness as they lay together, but the length wouldn't get caught underneath her when they tangled arms and legs.

Jordan let that image grow, reveling in the way his nerve endings seemed to be waking up.

Hope. He'd despaired of ever feeling that emotion again.

She moved her purse, revealing the way she filled out her blouse.

No model-skinny skeleton here.

Ample.

Just the way he liked them.

A flame of interest burned through the apathy he'd been living in these last months.

It felt good, and not just in his groin.

Want. Desire. The burning sensation in the pit of his solar plexus was a very good thing.

Need.

Not so good. He didn't need anyone.

"She said she was looking for Dr. Hart. When I pointed you out, she didn't seem to recognize you. Do you know her?"

Jordan shook his head. "Nope."

"Got any suspicions?"

Jordan ignored his cousin's curiosity, giving a strong stare at Rusty's bronc-riding vest instead. "You sure you want to do this?"

Not that Jordan didn't want to climb on a bucking bronc himself. Only, as the older cousin, he felt duty-bound to make a token protest after Rusty's last unsuccessful ride and consequent fall.

He refrained from rubbing his hand over his face.

He felt so old lately. And so numb.

"It's what we do, right?" Rusty shifted under Jordan's gaze. "Get thrown. Get right back on."

Jordan shook his head. "Until you get smart enough to realize you don't have to prove anything to anybody."

Unwanted sympathy showed in Rusty's eyes. "I guess you've had enough adrenaline rush to last a lifetime, huh?"

Jordan tightened his lips, neither confirming nor denying it.

He was supposed to be recovering from too much living on the edge. How could he admit to anyone that without that infusion of fight-or-flight-induced chemical his life was gray and deadly dull, bordering on meaningless?

His mare nudged him, clearly jealous when he should be paying attention to her. She didn't need words to make herself clear.

Absently, he reached up to scratch behind her ears. "No need to worry, Valkyrie. You're my best girl."

Rusty punched Jordan in his shoulder.

Jordan welcomed the pain to bring him back to himself.

"That's your problem, cuz. You've got women driving all the way out from who knows where to find you and you'd rather keep company with your horse." Rusty gave him a serious stare. "Get thrown. Get back on. That's what we do."

"Or wise up and learn I don't have to prove anything to anybody." With conviction, Jordan repeated his earlier statement, knowing neither he nor Rusty were talking about anything close to bull riding.

Rusty jostled him. "I'll say this about that city girl you brought us a few years ago. She tried. She really tried. You must have been doing something right for her to stay so long."

"What I was doing right was being a doctor. She was really impressed with that."

He ignored the worried look in Rusty's eyes and forced a grin to lighten the moment as he answered, "When she found out the only store within a fifty-mile radius was a combination feed store/hardware store/

boot shop with a smattering of jeans, hats and pearl button shirts to choose from, she quickly become disillusioned with small-town living."

Forcing those smiles was getting harder and harder.

"That was it? The lack of fancy department stores?" Rusty wasn't the first to try to pry out more information.

But a gentleman didn't kiss and tell. Jordan might not have a lot left going for him, but he was determined to keep his dignity.

He gave a self-deprecating shrug. "She loved boutiques more than me. I've learned to live with it."

"And you've had plenty of offers of companionship from the buckle bunnies to sooth any man's ego."

Jordan had to admit he'd taken advantage of enough of those offers that his ego should be well soothed.

But afterglow didn't last much past sunrise, did it?

He stole a quick glance at the woman in the stands. Should he recognize her?

"Old history." He leaned into Valkyrie, taking comfort in how the mare supported his weight. "I've grown up a bit since then."

As his shoulder throbbed where Rusty had punched him, he felt much older than his years.

Between the physical exertion he'd been doing to try to exhaust himself enough to sleep and the tossing and turning he'd done once he finally forced himself into bed, his bones hurt to the marrow.

Add that to his clinic schedule that had him working over sixty hours a week and he was starting to feel trapped in a dark tunnel as the light of the freight train bore toward him faster and faster.

What were the odds of finding a nurse practitioner who could take some of his load from him?

Over the loud speaker, the announcer called Rusty to the gate.

Jordan squared his shoulders. "Good luck."

"I don't need luck. Just a bull that wants to buck. Skill will take care of the rest." Rusty gave him a cocky grin then strutted toward the gates.

He watched his younger cousin with envy. What would it be like to feel alive again? To feel the blood rush through his veins? To feel his heart beat fast and his mind flash with lightning-quick thoughts? To feel a connection with another human being?

Although he tried to stop himself, he couldn't stop from glancing over at the woman staring intensely at him as if she were looking inside his head.

What did she see?

He pulled the brim of his hat lower and turned away, determined to ignore the feeling of being evaluated.

CHAPTER TWO

DESERÉ TOOK HER time studying Dr. Jordan Hart. Under cover of this crowd, there was no way he would notice a single pair of eyes trained on him. That she kept thinking he was glancing in her direction was purely her imagination as she never caught his eye, even though she tried.

He stood at least six feet one or two. His cowboy hat and boots made him look even taller. With his hat pulled low, she couldn't make out the color of his eyes or hair, but thought they might both be dark brown.

He was rangy with a stringy kind of muscle that would make his movements graceful.

As he shifted his weight, the chaps he wore emphasized his package. Modestly, she tried to look away, but her raging hormones wouldn't let her.

Something about being pregnant had kicked her libido into high gear. Whether it was because she no longer needed to worry about an accidental pregnancy or a release of hormones gone wild, or something else entirely, she couldn't tell for sure. She just knew that she was noticing men even more than she had during her intensely boy-crazy teenage years.

And she didn't want just sex. She wanted to be touched, petted, protected.

How many nights had she gone to sleep lately, pretending that her fantasy lover lay next to her, that he wrapped his arm around her and pulled her close, his big hand over her slightly softening belly?

Keeping this baby she carried hadn't been the original plan. But, then, the plan hadn't been for her sister to die, either.

Deseré pushed down her grief and straightened her spine. She was a survivor. Always had been. And always would be—especially now with her son to care for.

Her son.

Get a grip, Deseré. That's what her sister would have told her if she were here. *We do what we have to do to survive.*

That's what her sister had told her ten years ago as Deseré, acting as maid of honor, had arranged her sister's wedding veil so Celeste could walk down the aisle into the arms of the rich and powerful neurosurgeon who would provide for them both.

Deseré had thought that being a surrogate for Celeste would make up for some of the sacrifices her older sister had made for her. And it had, until Celeste had run a red light while talking on the phone and had crashed into an oncoming eighteen-wheeler.

Even though Deseré knew it was too early, she imagined baby James moving deep inside her.

She would do more than survive. She would build a happy, healthy life for her son and for herself.

In the indigo sky, the first star appeared opposite the fading sunset. Feeling foolish, she made a wish. *A miracle. Just a little one. Just a chance to prove myself, okay?*

A feeling of *be careful what you ask for* washed through her.

She shook it off. Fanciful and unrealistic things had no place in her practical world.

The reality was that everyone would say the politically correct thing. They would say her pregnancy didn't matter in her job hunt.

But the truth was no one wanted to hire a woman who would need time off to have a baby, not to mention time out of her workday for the morning sickness that struck like clockwork at ten a.m. each and every morning.

In less than a month her pregnancy would be evident. But by then she'd have had the job long enough to show her competence, long enough to make herself indispensable.

Her stomach lurched as she thought of how badly she needed this job.

With great willpower she stopped herself from staring at the man who could give her a safe, secure future.

Surely, her sister's husband, the great Dr. Santone, didn't have influence over every sleepy little town in Texas, did he?

What would a small-town country doctor care that a big-time surgeon who sat on the board of the largest hospital in Louisiana would be heartily upset if his sister-in-law found a job in the medical field?

Gathering her purse and slinging it over her shoulder, she pushed off the bench, remembering at the last moment to watch where she stepped as she walked toward Dr. Jordan Hart.

Feeling self-conscious, she looked up in time to see he was watching her every step of the way.

A challenge? Why?

Under the wide brim of his hat his eyes were too shaded by the darkening night skies to read. But his lips, so full and rich only a moment ago, were now set tight and grim.

"Dr. Hart?" Deseré called out.

"Just Jordan, ma'am." Automatically, Jordan touched the brim of his hat, not even thinking about it until he saw her eyes follow the movement of his hand.

She held out her hand. "Deseré Novak. Your new nurse practitioner."

Not a rodeo groupie at all. But she *was* an assertive little thing, wasn't she?

Dr. Wong's recommendation had seemed to contain a lot more between the lines than in black-and-white.

Dr. Wong hadn't exactly said she'd worked for him. The letter had been carefully worded. What Dr. Wong had said was that Deseré Novak deserved a chance.

So Jordan would give her one. But he'd only promised an interview.

Or did she think Dr. Wong's recommendations carried that much weight with him? Jordan was a man who made up his own mind about things.

"You're early for your interview. We didn't expect you until Monday."

She gave him a smile. "I thought I'd check out the place first."

"Makes sense." He put his hand in hers. "Thanks for coming to Piney Woods. I know we're a long way from New Orleans."

Her grip was firm. No-nonsense. Assertive. With just enough give to suggest hidden softness.

Ms. Novak's eyes flicked in worry before bravado had her lifting her chin. "I've already researched your practice. I'm sure it's perfect for me. You won't be sorry to hire me."

If Jordan hadn't noticed the slight quiver he would

have been fooled into thinking she was totally confident that she had the job.

It wasn't that he'd had any better-qualified applicants. How many experienced nurse practitioners wanted to move out to the edge of nowhere, taking room and board as a significant portion of their pay, when they could be pulling in the big bucks in any major city?

"We'll talk about it in the morning." He gestured to the open arena, still and quiet between events. "I've got other things going on tonight."

She stood still waiting for—for what?

Something about her stillness made him notice the dark circles under her eyes.

"The closest hotel is back toward Longview about two hours away. You may want to head in that direction before it gets much later."

She shook her head, shaking off his suggestion. "I understood room and board would be part of the deal. If you could point me toward this boarding house, maybe I could stay the night?"

"Boarding house." Jordan's smile was so tight it made his mouth hurt, way too tight to be reassuring, he was sure. "I guess, in a way, it is."

His office administrator had drawn up the job description.

It would be just like Nancy to gloss over the details to get what she wanted.

And what she wanted was a local medical facility for the folks of Piney Woods, solving two problems at once. The town and surrounding ranches would have good medical attention.

The loudspeaker blasted over the explanation he was about to give to clear up his office administrator's oversight.

Like everyone else in the stands, he turned to the gate to see his cousin poised over the back of a snorting and twisting bull.

Bull riding was a young man's sport. Rusty was getting too old for this.

But, then, his bullheaded cousin would probably realize that in the morning when he was too stiff to roll out of bed.

Jordan had been there, done that, got the belt buckle—and the scars—to prove it.

The woman next to him winced as she saw Rusty drop down onto the wide back of the bull.

Rusty settled in—as well as a man could settle onto the back of an angry bull—and gave a sharp nod.

The gate opened, the bull rushed out, and Jordan silently counted in his head, *one second, two seconds, three—*

And Rusty was off the bull and on the ground.

The rodeo clowns rushed in to distract the twenty-five-hundred-pound, four-legged kicking fury so Rusty could roll away from the dangerous hoofs.

Jordan squinted through the falling light, looking for that first twitch that said Rusty was going to catch his breath, jump up and walk out of the arena any second now.

"Come on, Rusty, shake it off," he murmured, as if saying it would send his cousin into action.

Dust hung in the air, as time stood still.

Rusty didn't move.

But the woman next to Jordan did.

She rushed toward the arena, looking like she intended to climb through the iron-pipe fence separating her from the bull.

Without thought, Jordan reached out and pulled her close to him.

"No." It came out harsh and uncompromising. It had been meant to. He'd been trained to give orders that were followed without question. He'd had too much practice to break the habit now.

There were a lot of habits he needed to work on breaking—like waking up in a cold sweat every night from his murky, twisted memory dreams. And jumping every time the barn door slammed closed, sounding too much like metal exploding.

And getting an adrenaline rush when he pulled a woman close to him to protect her from a non-existent danger.

Of course, she wasn't intending to go over the rail into an arena with an enraged bull running loose. Who in their right mind would?

His stomach sank as he had a surge of doubt in his ability to judge a situation. His instincts, which had always served him so well, might be a tad on the twisted side now.

A tad?

Still, he held her tightly pressed against his body as she struggled to get free, something deep inside him telling him to hold on tight and not let go.

Under other circumstances Jordan would have tried to defuse the situation by making a joke at his own expense, along with an apology as he sheepishly laughed off his rash and inappropriate behavior.

But his cousin lay facedown in the dirt, too still for too long, and Jordan had no words, much less a laugh.

"Let me go." She struggled against him. "Can't you see he needs help?"

Maybe his instincts weren't as far off as he'd thought they were.

Jordan gave a quick glance at the clowns as they herded the bull through the gate. One more second to make sure they latched it tight.

Then he let her loose, moved around her to put one boot on the top rung and vaulted over the fence racing toward Rusty with too many dire diagnoses running through his head for him to think straight.

As he knelt by his cousin's side, Deseré knelt on the other side. Had she gone over the top, too? Or squeezed between the rails? Did it matter? All that mattered was Rusty, lying so still. He was never still. But now…

Jordan felt frozen, inside and out.

Deseré was on her hands and knees, her silk shirt and slacks getting filthy as she tried to assess Rusty's state of consciousness.

Oh, God. Jordan thought it as a prayer, as cold dread started in the pit of his stomach, making its icy way to his heart. He hadn't even considered that Rusty might be…

"Unconscious," she said, her voice clipped.

She put her hand on Rusty's back, noting its rise and fall.

"Breathing," she reported.

Jordan nodded, realizing he'd been holding his own breath. Vacantly, he gazed down at his cousin's body, trying to get his own breathing regulated.

Worn, dusty boots stopped next to Jordan's knees. Jordan didn't know and didn't care who they belonged to.

With creaking knees Plato squatted down and touched Jordan's elbow. "Emergency Dispatch says the ambulances and paramedic crews are tied up. A truckload of teenagers tried to beat a train across the tracks. They don't know how long it will be. Do we need a chopper?" His calm voice, steady rheumy eyes and familiar wrinkled face piercing Jordan's fog.

Jordan tried to make the words make sense. The only thing getting through to him was that Rusty lay still, too still.

He put his hand on Rusty's back, willing him to take another breath.

"Dr. Hart?" Deseré prompted. "Authorize air transport?"

She nodded her head in the affirmative, giving him an obvious hint as to what his answer should be.

Jordan squeezed out a reply. "Yes."

How long had it been between the time Rusty had hit the ground and now? It seemed like hours. Or years. But it could have only been minutes. They would have called emergency services immediately, right?

His brain seemed to be thawing—finally. He was applying logic and making assumptions. Now he needed to apply that brain to Rus—to his patient. Thinking of his cousin as his patient would help him put some distance between his panic and his personal pain.

Vacantly, he noted that Deseré was positioning herself flat on her stomach, almost nose to nose with Rusty, something he should have already done.

"I'll stabilize his head while you check for spinal injuries," she said, stirring the churned-up dirt of the arena with her breath.

Jordan noted her technique. Thumbs on collarbone, fingers behind shoulders, Rusty's head firmly supported on her forearms. She definitely knew what she was doing.

She would be stuck like that until the emergency

crew arrived with their cervical collar and backboard and trained crew to whisk Rusty to the hospital in Longview, the closest trauma center but still twenty-five minutes away by air.

If the last ten minutes had seemed to be a decade, the next twenty-five would pass like centuries.

The way Deseré lay flat on her belly with her arms extended, holding Rusty tight to keep him immobile, breathing in the thick red dust, each minute must be torture.

Running his hands over Rusty's head then down, he started to check his cousin's spine carefully.

No weird angles. But that didn't mean much after the unnatural contortions Rusty's body had gone through while airborne.

As he got to mid-back, Rusty stirred.

"Tickles," he complained, as he tried to lift his face from the dirt.

But Jordan put one hand firmly on his lower hips and the other high on his back to hold him firmly in place.

"Be still," he growled, not caring about his lack of bedside manner.

"Can't. Back muscles are cramping."

"You can and you will. Be still while I finish checking to see if anything's broken."

Rusty lay still, as ordered.

Distantly Jordan noticed that his voice sounded fierce and uncompromising. Distantly, he also noticed his hands were following the correct path, searching for injuries.

Distantly. As if he was watching himself from a place not here, not now. As if his heart and soul weren't even connected to his mind or body. As if this wasn't his one and only cousin who he'd grown up with, shared camping trips with, shared double dates with and had left behind when he'd enlisted so the army would pay for his education all those years ago.

"Can you feel my hand on yours?" Jordan steeled himself to hear the wrong answer, going into total thinking mode and leaving no room for mind-clouding emotions like fear.

"Yeah, I can."

Holding his relief at bay, Jordan touched Rusty's other hand then both his calves above his boots. As Rusty gave an affirmative to each touch, Jordan felt his emotions continue to detach themselves.

Stoicism and survival—at least mental survival— went hand in hand. It was a lesson he'd apparently missed during his time in medical school but had discovered quickly enough for himself while in the field. Combat conditions had made him a fast learner.

In a meek, scared voice, Rusty asked, "Jordan, am I okay?"

"Just checking you out, Rust Bucket." From that place far remote from him where he'd left his emotions, Jordan knew calling his cousin by his detested nickname would be reassuring. Until the hospital's helicopter arrived, soothing the patient was all he could do.

The patient. Jordan lumped Rusty in with the thousands of patients he'd treated. He wouldn't allow himself to connect, wouldn't allow himself to care. Not here. Not now.

Maybe that other Jordan, the one who seemed so far away from him right now, was caring. But all this Jordan felt was numb. And efficient.

Being efficient was critical.

Maybe later he could feel.

Or maybe later would never come.

But none of that mattered right now.

Finally, after he'd lost count of the breaths he'd begun to count in and out, he heard the helicopter land in the dark clearing where someone had set out flares.

As the paramedic crew got into place with their backboard and cervical collar and their professionalism, he heard himself give them a succinct account of the accident, of Rusty's state of consciousness, of his initial findings of a possible broken arm and of Rusty's pain level.

And the pain of Rusty, lying facedown in the dirt, hit him in the heart.

Too late, he remembered that numbness was better.

Still on his knees, he moved back, getting out of a paramedic's way so he could do his job.

Desperately, he grasped for that numbness before it could slip away.

Instead, he could only kneel there in the dirt as he fought back the moisture that blurred his vision.

How many times had he knelt at the side of young men and women while he'd served his time in Afghanistan as they'd waited to be airlifted to safety? As if any place over there had felt safe.

Now was not the time to think of that.

Not now. Not ever, if he could keep pushing all those memories back.

Any second now he would find the strength, the motivation to stand.

He just needed to shore up his personal dam and everything would be fine.

Deseré stood next to him. When had she relinquished her position to the paramedic? When the paramedic had slipped the collar on and loaded Rusty onto the backboard, of course.

She put her hand on his shoulder, a firm touch followed by a squeeze.

And just like that he didn't feel so alone, so isolated, so *solely* responsible.

As if Deseré's voice had breached the invisible wall around him, he heard her tell the paramedics, "We'll notify his family."

That's when he realized they had been speaking to him, asking him questions about next of kin, giving him information about where they were taking Rusty and how to contact the hospital for updates.

How many times had he spoken with families, giving them the same kind of information? Only he'd had to talk via phone to loved ones who had been continents away, speaking into an unsympathetic piece of plastic in his hand as he'd explained that their soldier had lost hands or eyes or legs.

He'd heard everything from silence to deep soulful keening over those invisible airwaves. Each response had burned itself into his mind.

How long would he fight the memories?

A paramedic knelt next to him, gently jostling him. "We've got the patient, Dr. Hart."

How long had he knelt there, in the way?

Too long, even if it had only been for a few seconds.

He stood and backed away. From somewhere outside himself, he said, "I'll follow in my truck."

One of the rodeo clowns, who had been standing behind him and whom he'd been vaguely aware of, though he didn't seem to belong in this scene with his brightly painted face, baggy clothes and suspenders, said quietly, "Jordan, you're our medical professional on duty. We'll have to shut down the event if you leave. I understand about Rusty and all, but there are some big purses and points on the line here."

Jordan looked over at the woman with the ruined pants and blouse, filthy, too-delicate shoes and streaks of dirt on her cheek.

As if he were standing beside himself, watching, he saw himself lift his hand and wipe at a streak near her mouth with his thumb.

Her eyes deepened into a dark navy as she froze. She didn't even blink. Just looked at him like a deer in the headlights, too stunned to run away.

Embarrassment dropped him back into himself as he realized what he'd done.

He clenched his fist as he focused on the problem at hand and made his decision. "My nurse practitioner will take over my duties here."

He looked up, spotting Plato and Sissy, and motioned them over.

"Deseré Novak, meet Plato, my ranch help, and Sissy Hart, my sister and resident veterinarian. Ms. Novak will be taking over in my absence. Plato will introduce you around and show you the medical supplies. Sissy will make sure you have a place to stay tonight." He paused, looking into each of their faces. "Any questions?"

Plato swiped his hand over his face. "You can take the officer out of the military, but you can't..." He let the rest of his statement trail off under Jordan's glare.

Beside him, Deseré was nodding her acceptance as if nothing could ruffle her composure.

Sissy frowned. "Jordan, where—?"

Jordan looked at the lights of the helicopter growing dimmer in the sky. "Call Nancy. This is her mess."

"We've got this, Doctor." Deseré gave him a calm, if tight smile. "Go do what you need to do."

As if two massive boulders had fallen from his shoulders, Jordan felt energy course through him, the energy he needed to make it through tonight.

"Thanks." Emotion had him sounding gruffer than he had intended.

Deseré didn't seem to mind. "You're welcome. Now go."

Ignoring the shocked expressions on Sissy's and Plato's faces, Jordan took long, quick strides toward his truck as the helicopter lifted off, strobing bright light into the darkening sky.

As he climbed into his truck, he thought he should have nagging guilt about deserting his post. Instead, he felt comfort, deep down from the place where his instincts were born.

He was no longer alone.

For the first time in a very long time he could feel the tight, invisible bands around his chest loosen enough to let him draw in a deep breath.

The feeling of relief was seductive and he wanted to breathe in more.

But he couldn't forget—wouldn't forget—that letting down his guard created a sure-fire path to disappointment and bone-crushing pain.

CHAPTER THREE

WATCHING DR. HART stride away, stretching out his steps, going over the pipe-rail fence in one fluid motion, making the most of those incredibly long, lean legs of his while seeming to be unhurried and in control, left Deseré feeling lost and alone.

But wasn't that her status quo with men?

Not that Dr. Hart was a— Of course he was a man, but he wasn't a relationship or a potential relationship, except purely in the professional sense.

And that's the only sense she needed. Except for her common sense, which she seemed to have misplaced.

My nurse practitioner, Dr. Jordan had said. That meant she was hired, right?

She hadn't been able to acknowledge her worries and doubt before, not even to herself, but now she could admit to herself that she'd had no other options if this one hadn't worked out.

Going back the way she had come hadn't been an option. She'd never been afraid of any man. Cautious, sure. Wary, always. But not out-and-out afraid.

Not until her brother-in-law had sidled up to her at her sister's funeral and said he'd made arrangements out of state for an off-the-books abortion. They could call it a miscarriage, blaming it on grief.

When she'd refused, she'd seen pure evil in his eyes.

As time had passed, he'd changed his tune, deciding Deseré would take her sister's place as mother to the child that wasn't biologically his—and in his bed. He'd had it all figured out in that twisted mind of his, even down to the admiration of his friends when he'd magnanimously taken on the responsibility of his dead wife's sister.

An icy chill ran down her spine as she remembered his threats, the least of which had been unemployment as he'd tried to wreck her financially so she would have to comply with his plans.

Her brother-in-law had made it very clear she would never work in New Orleans again. And the interviews she'd had at all the major hospitals in Louisiana, Mississippi and most of Texas had emphasized the reach of his power.

Thankfully, he had forgotten this tiny fly speck on the map. Hopefully, he'd never find it.

"Ma'am? I'm Plato." The old cowboy she'd first seen in the parking lot was at her side. He tipped his hat as he officially introduced himself.

Deseré figured that meant something, some kind of acceptance into this world of boots and spurs.

"Deseré Novak." She held out her dirty hand then tried to pull it back. "Sorry."

He took her hand in his. His gnarled knuckles stood out as he gave her a light but firm pressure. "No, ma'am. The way I see it, that's angel dust coating your hand, not dirt. What you did for Rusty, well…" He rubbed his eyes with the back of his hand before he cleared his throat. "I'm sure one of the girls could come up with something for you to wear, if you wanted to change."

Deseré looked down at her blouse and slacks, covered in red-tinged dust. "It's a good thing I'm not a dry cleaning-only kind of woman."

She brushed at her pants leg and her hand became as dirt-coated as her pants. Not that her hands or arms were especially clean after she'd lain on her belly in the dirt, stabilizing Rusty's head and neck. She probably had red dirt all over her face, too.

Plato gave her a rueful look. "We've got iron ore in our soil around here." He pointed to her pants. "That might not come out."

Deseré categorized her limited wardrobe. Three pairs of slacks, two blouses, a set of very washed and worn scrubs, one little black dress inherited from her sister's closet, a pair of jeans with the waistband already too snug, a pair of sweats and three oversize T-shirts she slept in.

"I've got it covered." She turned to head toward her car in the parking lot but all she saw was a solid ring of pipe fencing.

And bleachers full of people watching her every move as she stood under the bright arena lights.

As she moved, the crowd erupted into cheers.

For her? She'd only done what any medical professional would have done.

Her heart beat as if pure energy surged through it instead of blood as she soaked in the approval. It had been so long since she'd felt like anyone was on her side. And now bleachers full of strangers were cheering her on.

It felt good, but overwhelming at the same time.

"This way, ma'am." Plato put his hand on her elbow, making her feel like rodeo royalty.

Cowgirl princess had always been a fantasy of hers. But her cowboy prince had already left the arena.

Her cowboy prince? It must be the adrenaline swing,

the sleepless nights—her stomach growled—and the hunger getting to her.

She didn't believe in princes on white horses rescuing damsels in distress. She didn't believe in damsels in distress, either. All she believed in was herself—and some days that was hard enough, without trying to add fairy-tales to the mix.

As they reached a part of the fence that looked as solid as every other part, Plato swung a gate open. It creaked and squealed on its hinges, proving it didn't get much use.

A woman in her forties, or well-preserved fifties, with big white-blonde hair and huge diamonds at her ears, neck and fingers, met her at the gate. She could have been the mother of any of the blonde cowgirls now crowding the rail.

"I'm Gayle-Anne." Her smile was orthodontia perfect. "Honey, you can use my trailer to change in. It's not very big but it's private."

Deseré bet it was a lot bigger than the bathroom stall at the discount department store where she'd last changed.

"Thanks. I'll just get clean clothes from my car."

If the woman wondered why Deseré had a wardrobe change in her car, she was polite enough not to ask about it.

How long did rodeos last? Hours?

Squeezing into her tight jeans had no appeal, especially if she was going to be stuck on one of those wooden benches for any length of time.

Too tired to give fashion decisions any more thought, she unzipped her bag and grabbed the first thing that came to hand, her sweats and a T-shirt.

The promise of comfort more than made up for her lack of ability to make a better decision.

Digging into the bottom of the bag, she snagged her tennis shoes and exchanged them for her useless sandals. The beat-up shoes had seen better days but, then, so had she.

And so had Jordan Hart.

She might have been the one lying in the dirt, but he was the one walking through hell. She'd seen it in his eyes as he'd gazed down at his cousin. Being a stoic medical professional worked just fine until it was someone close to you who needed your care.

She'd felt so helpless. So useless. The only thing she'd been able to do for her sister had been to promise to take care of her baby, a promise she'd given without reservation, then had had to fight dirty to keep.

She didn't regret the loss of her home or her career even a fraction as much as she grieved the loss of her sister.

Inside, baby James moved. Everyone would tell her that he was too small to feel, but they would all be wrong. She might not feel his tiny body, but she felt his great soul inside her.

She would keep her promise. She'd given her word.

And right now her word was the only significant thing she had to call her own.

Jordan paced the hallway, waiting, waiting. X-ray. CT scan. Radiologist report.

Rusty.

And the woman he'd left behind. What had he done, hiring her like that? Being impulsive wasn't like him. Had never been like him.

While it was true that he hadn't been himself in a while now, had he completely lost his mind?

He stopped pacing. Maybe.

Pain arced through him, starting in his heart and spreading through his veins. The pain of fear.

Not now. Now was not the time to have a panic attack.

Through sheer force of will he made himself start walking again. Walk. Breathe. Don't think.

Don't think about the woman waiting at his house, confused. Needing a job. Desperate.

He'd seen it in her eyes.

What had she seen in his?

Deseré's back screamed in pain from sitting on that hard wooden bench so long and her stomach burned with indigestion that had to rival the pits of hell.

The old cowboy had brought her a hot dog and a Frito pie, both covered in spicy chili, apologizing that this was all the little makeshift food stand had to offer.

She'd eaten them, of course. Even if she hadn't been starving, turning down free food would have been foolish in her financial situation.

But now, if she could go back in time, she probably would have done the same thing. Heartburn would eventually fade away and she needed the calories and scant nutrients the food provided.

As for going back in time—if she had that ability, she'd certainly take herself back a lot further than a few hours ago.

But how far back? Back before their father had died in Hurricane Katrina's flooding and Celeste had taken on the responsibility of raising her younger sister? Would that be far enough back?

What part of her history would she be willing to accept as her starting point for life?

Here and now. That's all she had. That's all she'd ever had.

But Dr. Hart had given her a future. *My nurse practitioner*, he'd said, giving her his stamp of approval, his acceptance and his protection all in one hasty pronouncement.

In a small community like this, everything he'd said and done was significant. Even now, she'd bet plenty of folks were dissecting and discussing every nuance.

Even after she was invited to the announcers' booth, their flimsy metal chairs weren't an improvement over the hard wooden benches and the staleness of the booth, the odor of burnt coffee mixed with dust and sweat that had built up over the years made her stomach roil.

She swatted at a gnat on her neck, one of millions in league with the mosquitoes that flocked to taste any sliver of exposed skin.

She'd opted to sit outside as the night air brought the heat and humidity down a few degrees. The perspiration soaking her shirt chilled her, making her shiver.

And she was so tired she was having difficulty deciding if she was awake or asleep. She wrapped her arms around herself, surprised to find a blue jean jacket awkwardly draped around her chair and over her shoulders.

That answered it. She'd been asleep—asleep enough that she was startled when the older cowboy, the one she recognized from the parking lot, cleared his throat.

"Ma'am?" Plato's volume, a touch above a normal speaking voice, firm but still calm and gentle, clued her in that this wasn't the first time he'd tried to awaken her.

She blinked, trying to bring his leathered face into focus.

Pasting on the best smile she could, even though it felt extremely weak to her, she answered in kind, "Sir?"

Relief showed in his rheumy blue eyes.

Cataracts? Glaucoma? The medical professional started to evaluate diagnoses.

But the exhausted woman overruled them, appreciating the concern and sympathy she found in those bloodshot, yellow-tinged eyes.

"Ready to go home now?" His words made his rough voice sound sweeter than any angel's song.

Home. Had she finally found home?

"Yes." Awkwardly, she gathered her purse, trying to hold the jacket around her shoulders while she wiggled functionality into her swollen feet.

He reached out for her.

As an independent woman, she usually waved away the courtesy.

But tonight, his hand on her elbow, guiding her, steadying her, gave her more comfort than she would ever have imagined.

Gratefully and graciously, she accepted the other hand he held out for her as she made the step from the second-row bleacher to the ground.

"You can follow Sissy, or I can drive your car for you and catch a ride back here for my truck."

Her car. All that she owned was in that car. The stark reality was enough to push away the blanket of sleep that weakened her.

Her brain jump-started and she remembered who Sissy was—Jordan's sister.

Jordan. When had he become Jordan in her head instead of Dr. Hart?

"I'll follow Sissy."

* * *

Deseré should have let the old man drive her.

Bleary-eyed, she slammed on her brakes and slowed enough to just miss the bumper of Sissy's truck as the vet turned off the two-lane road onto a crumbling black-topped street that had deteriorated on the edges so that it was only the width of a car and a half.

Carefully, she put distance between her car and the truck in front of her, on alert for sudden brake lights.

And her caution was validated when Sissy slowed her truck to a crawl and turned into a dirt and gravel drive without bothering to use her blinkers first.

Trees crowded the driveway—and Deseré used the description of driveway very loosely. How far away from the street was the house?

And then they turned a steep curve and there it was, a farmhouse that could have come from a movie set, or her dreams.

Headlights showed a huge, two-storied, white-painted wooden house with gray shingles and a darker gray double door centered under a deep covered wrap-around porch. Rocking chairs promised the good life once the grimy cushions were replaced and they were swept clear of cobwebs.

If Deseré had to pick out the perfect picture of a po-tential home, this would be it.

Which meant she immediately put herself on guard.

Nothing was this easy. This neat. This perfect.

Where was the catch?

Ahead of her, Sissy had her arm stuck out her truck's window as she wildly gestured to an empty carport that branched off from the drive.

Deseré interpreted that to mean, "Park here." She could always move it later if she was wrong.

She pulled into the expansive parking place, taking up most of the room by sloppily not squaring her car with the open space. The lack of order felt off, but not as off as her head, which chose that moment to swim in that dizzy, depleted way that meant she'd gone as far as she could today.

Sissy inspected her parking job and clearly found it lacking. With a frown, she shrugged and said, "Jordan will just have to deal with it."

Deseré knew she should ask for clarification but right now she didn't really want to know. Knowing might mean exerting more energy than she had to give.

Grabbing her backpack and wriggling her arms through the straps, she breathed deeply to gather her strength for wrestling her rolling suitcase from the back seat.

"Since Jordan has hired you *sans* interview, Nancy said to bring you here and she would get everything sorted out later." Sissy swept her hand to indicate the house before her. "Home, sweet home."

Deseré felt like Sissy was waiting for a reply.

"It's large," she answered politely, reserving judgment until she saw the inside of the house.

Sissy nudged her aside and pulled the suitcase out for her, handling it like it was full of popcorn. "I'll carry this one for you."

Normally, Deseré would have protested, but she didn't have it in her. Instead, she muttered a tired "Thanks" and pulled her purse and smaller duffel bag from the front seat of the car.

On autopilot, she followed Sissy up the three steps to the front porch then through the wooden and etched-glass front door.

Sissy paused as she looked down the short wing to

the left then up to the second floor. She bit her lower lip and her brow creased as she seemed to be puzzling out a dilemma. "I'm not sure where to put you."

"Anywhere is fine." Deseré mustered up a polite smile, wondering how many other tenants shared the boarding house.

Sissy quit deliberating and nodded her head. "Okay, then. This way." She headed up a staircase lit with just enough wall sconces to cast shadows on the floral patterned carpet runner covering each oak-plank step, dragging Deseré's large suitcase over each one.

Deseré didn't need to respond. She would only have been talking to Sissy's back. Instead, she meekly followed the diminutive woman hefting the large suitcase to the end of the hallway to the left.

Sissy swung open the last door to reveal a bedroom. The room was enormous, bigger than the whole living room and den combination in Deseré's old apartment.

The sight of that luxurious bed put the rest of the room into the background. A huge queen-size bed held a half-dozen big pillows propped against the headboard and the promise of sweet dreams.

A calming lavender color scheme and trophies and blue ribbons displayed on every inch of shelf space gave the room a mixed attitude of super-girly but highly competitive.

"This was my room before I moved out. I should probably pack up some of this stuff, huh? But the closet's cleared out so at least you can unpack." She pointed to a closed door next to a substantial desk. "The bathroom's through that door."

Sissy dumped the suitcase outside the bifold louvered doors of a closet then shoved aside a group of trophies on a wide chest of drawers, took Deserés duffel bag from her and plopped it onto the cleared space.

An unexpected expression of doubt crossed Sissy's eyes. "I hope this will do."

"It's great." Deseré didn't need to dredge up a fake smile. It came quite naturally as she emphasized her answer. "Really. It's wonderful."

"Well, okay, then." Sissy looked out into the hallway, obviously ready to make her exit. "I'm sure Jordan will straighten out any questions you might have in the morning."

Absently, Deseré nodded, wishing Sissy would leave. Falling into that lovely bed and stretching out her back was the only thing she wanted to straighten out right now.

"Good night, then." Sissy didn't wait for a reply. Her duty done, she started out the bedroom door.

"Good night," Deseré said to Sissy's retreating backside, then closed the door as soon as she thought it polite to do so.

Her first inclination was to fall into that bed and sleep for a week. But her mouth had a sour taste that couldn't be ignored and grit coated her face and hands.

Cleanliness warred with exhaustion. A quick wash-up would be worth the extra time and energy.

Opening the solid door next to the desk, Deseré was sure she'd opened the door to bathroom heaven.

The modernized bathroom was the size of a normal bedroom, with two basins and a huge vanity. The size of each of the basins put the discount store's basins she'd been spot-bathing in to shame. A wall-to-wall mirror hung over the vanity, reflecting the light from nickel-plated fixtures that caught the atmosphere of farmhouse yet produced enough light for professional make-up application.

An alcove held the toilet separately from the frosted glass doors, which must hide the shower enclosure.

Immediately, every inch of skin on Deseré's body wanted scrubbing. She couldn't stop herself from wondering where Jordan would be showering tonight. Would anyone be washing his back?

How could her libido be so wide-awake when the rest of her was practically sleepwalking?

Because she couldn't help herself, she opened the frosted door to inspect the shower.

Oh, my. She had no doubt she had entered an entirely different world than the one she had come from.

With three shower heads embedded in each wall of the hexagon-shaped shower and a marble bench wide and deep enough to lie down on, the shower was big enough to hold an orgy in.

Hedonistic didn't begin to cover it.

With no further thought needed, Deseré stripped off her filthy clothes, grabbed a towel and washcloth from the cabinets under the vanity and jumped in to adjust the temperature and spray.

Five minutes later, she stood in the middle of the multiple streams of steaming water. Each spray felt like firm fingers massaging her skin, pulsating against her sore muscles, sending slick, soapy water sluicing from head to toe.

Better than sleep.

Better than sex.

The phrases kept going through her head like a seductive song as she stretched and soaped and rinsed and soaped again, washing away all the demoralizing spot baths she'd taken with paper towels and harsh pink antibacterial soap while hiding in public toilet stalls.

The soap smelled of cedar and sage. The shampoo held a hint of musk. The masculine tinge only underscored the sensual feel of the spray tingling against her skin.

What would it be like to make love in this shower?

That was a very improper thought for an expectant mother.

Determined to shrug off her fantasies, she squirted another handful of shampoo into her palm to work it through her hair and into her scalp.

Ah. Heaven.

Through her sudsing and soaping and spraying, she had the vague notion she might have heard the bathroom door swing open.

No, she was not going to let a little paranoia invade this moment of bliss.

Instead, she let the fancy shower heads push pulsating fingers of hot water into her spine as she stretched, reaching far, far over her head, reaching for the stars.

Her moan of sheer pleasure echoed in the cavernous shower.

She grabbed her wet hair, intending to flop over at the waist and wash away the shampoo while she stretched in the opposite direction, when she heard him.

"What the hell?"

Despite the rich, thick shampoo bubbles filling her ears, Jordan Hart's voice came through loud and clear.

CHAPTER FOUR

As JORDAN PUSHED the bathroom door open, worry for Rusty gave way to reality and the sound of the shower running.

"Um— Hello? Is someone out there?" Her voice was breathy, reminding Jordan too much of mornings-after he hadn't experienced in too long.

"I— Uh." Now was not the time to have his brain go blank as his world unfolded in slow motion.

For the first time in a very, very long time Jordan felt like a teenager caught in the back seat of his girlfriend's car. Two parts shocked, one part guilty and another part as excited as a lightning bolt.

She turned away from him, giving him a foggy view of her backside.

Hell, make that a whole lightning storm raging through him. He clenched and unclenched his fists.

"Uh, would you get out now, please?" Her whispery voice breached his confusion. It broke, sounding scared, making him feel big and hulking and embarrassed.

Making him feel.

His numbness washed away like soap scum down the drain.

"Sorry," he said, and headed for the door that connected to his bedroom, firmly closing it behind him.

Sleeping was difficult at the best of times.

No way would he get any rest with every nerve ending in his body popping.

Kicking off his jeans and boots, he pulled on shorts and running shoes instead. As he slammed out the door and hit the road, a full range of emotions hit him.

After being safely numb for so long, reaction after delayed reaction now threatened to bring him to his knees.

Lust for the woman who was now his employee and, therefore, hands off. Relief that Rusty was going to be fine. Pressure of caring for his heavy patient load when he couldn't even care for himself.

And fear that all the emotion he had under such tight control, all the guilt and angst and anger would finally burst free, consuming him and everyone around him.

If only he could run far enough, fast enough...

If only he could outrun the agony of feeling again that dogged his every step.

Nothing like being walked in on by your boss, a man you'd only met a few short hours ago, to jumpstart your heart.

Deseré used her newfound energy to grab her towel, lock the door she hadn't noticed opposite the one that led into her bedroom and, for good measure, lock her door, too, all in under three seconds.

Keeping one towel tightly around her and tucked under her armpits, she grabbed a second one, toweled off her legs and arms and then squeezed the water from her hair, letting her mind settle from flight mode into thinking mode.

A second door meant a second bedroom, right?

Shampoo and soap... She opened the drawer under

both basins—used toothbrush and a squeezed tube of toothpaste, deodorant and a man's electric razor. A full bottle of cologne covered with dust. And an opened box of condoms.

She would not peek inside to see how many were left. It was none of her business.

Did she really think a man who looked like him, a man who walked like him, who talked like him, each word so slow and deep it rumbled with masculinity, would be celibate?

Again, what did it matter to her?

So they shared a bathroom.

She took another look at the luxurious shower.

She could deal with it.

She'd shared living quarters, including a bathroom, with a man before. But that man hadn't been the slightest bit interested in her—not when her sister had been sharing his bed.

If only Celeste had stuck with that particular boyfriend instead of dumping him for money…

But who could have predicted this future?

Once again she pushed down her grief for her sister. She'd done her crying when she'd heard the news. All it had done was make her sick at her stomach.

Crying solved nothing. Thinking, planning then taking action was the way to move forward.

Whatever you do, don't stand still, Deseré. Moving targets are harder to hit. Celeste had always felt safer on the move, dragging them both from boyfriend to homeless shelter to a room over the garage in exchange for babysitting services.

But she wanted more for Celeste's son—her son— than a life on the run.

And, like her sister before her, she would never lose hope.

A chill shook her as the overhead vents blew centralized air conditioning onto her damp skin.

Still wet under the tightly wrapped towel, she cringed at the thought of putting on the filthy clothes she'd shed when she'd made the spontaneous decision to explore the wonders of that magnificent shower.

Scrubs it would be.

And tomorrow she would avail herself of the washer and dryer.

With the beginning of the weekend, she would have a chance to wash and dry out the wrinkles before donning them for work on Monday and she would also have a chance to scope out her surroundings, both the town and the office, and begin working on fitting in.

Most importantly, she would have a chance to get that awkward encounter with her boss behind her.

The sooner, the better.

Because she wasn't going anywhere.

Anywhere but bed.

After pulling on her scrubs and unlocking the connecting doors, she allowed herself to pull back the duvet on the huge, beautiful bed that dominated the room.

Sure that she would lie awake spending hours thinking about today and tomorrow and yesterday, at least she would do it in comfort.

But the moment she lay down among the half-dozen pillows and stretched out to her full length, exhaustion overtook her.

As her world went sleepily hazy, she reached out for a pillow, wondering what it would be like to encounter a warm male body instead. A body like Jordan Hart's.

* * *

Jordan cranked up the volume as music blasted through his earbuds. The vintage rock classic about running down the road, trying to loosen his load, fit the situation perfectly except for the part about seven women on his mind. He only had one woman on his mind.

And no matter how hard he pushed his pace, he couldn't outrun her steamy, naked body in his shower.

His imagination wanted to take off where his memory ended.

And he let it.

Would he feel electricity in her touch?

Or would he feel nothing.

Nothing. Nothing. Nothing.

It became his mantra superimposed over the music in his ears as he made his way back home.

Home became interspersed in his internal chant.

Nothing.

Home.

Nothing.

Home.

Nothing.

The trance he'd set out to find finally wrapped itself around him as his stride became a part of his breath, a part of his world, a world that only encompassed his next step.

He gasped for breath, realizing he'd been sprinting full out instead of at his long-distance endurance pace.

The pounding of his heart competed with the throbbing in his chest.

Physical pain.

Bringing him back to here and now, reminding him that, no matter how fast or how far he ran, he could never outrun reality.

He climbed the front steps of his porch, unlocking his front door as silently as he could manage, creeping up the stairs, stepping over the fifth step that had creaked since his youth and headed for a shower—a cold one where he would fight his memories, fight the imaginary world of what-if, fight his inclination to keep on running.

And remember why he was there. Why the clinic was so important. Why he couldn't just check out, no matter how seductive that thought was.

As he had a hundred thousand times before, to too many unanswered questions, he raised his face to the stream of water pouring down on him and silently pleaded, Why?

Deseré woke up slowly, drowsily, until she was awake enough to be confused.

Spread across the huge, soft bed, she began to remember.

The rodeo.

Jordan.

The bull-riding accident.

Jordan.

This house.

And Jordan.

Walking in on her in the shower. Seeing her naked. Turning away.

Which had been the right thing to do.

Anything else would have been creepy. Scary. Dangerous.

Those words didn't go with Jordan Hart.

At least the creepy, scary words didn't.

Dangerous?

Something about him hinted that he could be. But he would never harm her.

How could she know that about him? He was a stranger, a man she'd just met only briefly under trying circumstances.

She knew nothing about him.

But she knew, deep down, that he would never hurt her.

She had that sense, too well developed over too many years, that told her which man was dangerous and which was safe.

Jordan. A dangerous thrill shivered down her spine.

No, he wouldn't hurt her. At least, not physically. What that man could do to a woman's psyche was another matter entirely.

And her heart?

Deseré pushed that thought away. No man would ever get close to her heart unless she allowed it. And she definitely hadn't been in a permissive mood lately.

The urge that had woken her hit her with an intensity that had her sitting up in bed.

Bathroom.

Oh, the luxury of having one right outside her bedroom door.

Using moon shadows to navigate, she padded across the room—to find the connecting door locked from the bathroom side.

The sound of water running at full blast made her instinctively twitch.

Knowing Jordan was showering on the other side of this door made her twitch even more.

He's a stranger, she reminded herself.

But she'd seen beyond his socially acceptable stranger's mask.

She'd seen his eyes as he'd looked down at his cousin.

She'd seen his eyes as he'd stared at her in the foggy mirror.

She'd seen his eyes as he'd turned away.

She'd seen that glimpse of emotion that could only be his soul.

Deseré shook herself, shaking off her high-drama fantasy.

It was not like her to wax poetic over a man's eyes.

She had never been one of those girls who fell in love with the idea of love the second she laid eyes on an attractive guy.

Practical. Realistic. Survivor.

That's what she was.

Pregnancy hormones. What other reason could it be?

Finally, just when she thought she would have to go in search of a second bathroom in an unfamiliar house, she heard the shower shut off, heard the bathroom door open—

And jiggled her own doorhandle, only to find it still locked.

What?

Had he forgotten to unlock the connecting door?

So, her choices were limited, both in option and in the time factor. She could pound on his bedroom door or she could find another bathroom.

Remembering their last encounter in this very bathroom, Deseré choose option two.

Barefoot, she sprinted toward the stairs, using memory more than vision. No windows? Not enough moon to cast a glow?

Not an issue to ponder now. Maybe she should have gone with option one.

No, she still had time.

As she hopped from foot to foot, her hand swept the wall near the first step.

Light switch? Light switch?

No light switch.

Holding onto the stair rail, Deseré took each step as cautiously as she could while making maximum haste.

She really should have just knocked on his door.

But with only two steps left, turning around now would take too much time.

Really, I love you, baby James. But sometimes you make Momma's thinking process short-circuit.

Momma.

She'd never called herself that before. As dire as her need was, she had to stop for a moment.

"Momma," she said aloud, making it real. She was going to me a mother. Responsible for this fragile life inside her until he reached manhood.

She couldn't imagine letting go even then.

The wonder of it all was so big it momentarily distracted her from her mission.

But then cool air swirled around her as the air-conditioner kicked in and the importance of finding a bathroom became very important.

Opening the door under the staircase, she found a closet full of winter coats. The closet smelled of mustiness and—and Jordan.

Jordan, who she was going to great pains to avoid. Jordan, who she would see in the morning anyway.

Jordan, on whose bedroom door she should have knocked instead of putting herself through this wild-goose chase.

Jordan, who she had just dreamed about in a way that would make seeing him in the light of day awkward.

Seeing him tonight in his bedroom, feeling sleepy and vulnerable, would have been much worse.

She had made the right decision.

Her bladder twinged.

Maybe.

Another door yielded a bedroom in disrepair, spooky in the shadows coming through the curtainless windows. Drop cloths draped the floor and furniture, turning everything into ghosts. But a small open doorway gave her a glimpse of white tile.

Yes!

Quickly, she picked her way through the paint-brushes and wallpaper rolls to come face-to-face with a toilet that lay on its side, awaiting installation.

That. Hurt.

She turned on her heel, stepping on a roller and almost going to her knees.

Steadying herself on the corner of a dresser-shaped ghost, she regained her balance.

Enough of this. What was the big deal, knocking on Jordan Hart's door?

Seeing him fresh from his bed.

Would his hair be mussed, as if a lover's fingers had just run through it?

Would his mouth be full, relaxed from a deep sleep?

Would his eyes—those wonderful eyes—be slightly unfocused as he blinked the sleep away?

Option one. It's all she had left.

She raced up the stairs as fast as she could manage.

Outside his door, she raised her hand and knocked.

CHAPTER FIVE

As she waited for Jordan to answer her knock, Deseré felt like one of those too-stupid-to-live teenage girls in a cheesy horror flick who goes into the dark basement defenseless and too dumb to be scared.

Not that she had any reason to fear Jordan Hart if her instincts were right. And they had never failed her before.

But, then, she'd never been suffused with pregnancy hormones before, either.

Realistically, she didn't know the man. And she was all alone with him.

Her desperate search for a bathroom had confirmed that there were no other residents. This wasn't a boarding house but a private home. A home that only she and Jordan presently occupied.

But plenty of people knew where she was, right?

No. Wrong. Only his sister and the old cowboy Plato and a woman named Nancy, whom she had never met.

She shifted from foot to foot and pounded again, impatiently waiting for him to open that door. The sooner the better. Right?

Or not so right?

What a great time to get scared—or get smart.

She had an absurd vision of Plato leaning on a shovel, peering down into a freshly dug—

Jordan answered the door, a look of total blankness on his face. "You need something?"

His lack of emotion unsettled her more than a frown or a scowl would have. That and the way his gym shorts showed off his muscular legs. His worn T-shirt draped across his wide shoulders. His uncombed hair fell onto his forehead, creating the illusion of vulnerability.

Deseré swallowed. Her dry throat made it painful. She was staring at him, staring at his face, staring into his eyes and seeing nothing but flat black pupils surrounded by whiskey-brown with specks of black.

"Well?" His voice was firm and solid and impatient. That vulnerability thing was definitely an illusion.

He blinked.

Was that a touch of wariness he blinked away?

"Bathroom." She pointed, unable to put any other thoughts into words.

His body shifted, giving her the impression he was moving back from the door to let her in.

She couldn't wait anymore.

Brushing against him, she headed for that little slice of heaven she needed so desperately.

Anyone would think that her single-minded mission would block everything else from her world. How did the heat of his arm against hers stand out from all the other things she was feeling?

Slamming the bathroom door a little harder than she'd intended, Deseré fumbled with the lock, hoping it caught, then found blessed relief.

As she washed her hands, she debated her next move, even while shaking her head at the silliness of letting something as simple as using the bathroom get so out blown out of proportion in her mind.

But she couldn't help it.

Jordan Hart was larger than life. Wait—she meant he was crucial to her life, not larger than life.

He was an ordinary man. Nothing special. Nothing scary.

But he did scare her. Not in the axe-murderer kind of way but in the change-her-life kind of way.

Rolling her eyes at herself in the mirror, she dried her hands on the hand towel more roughly than was warranted.

This wasn't a big deal. She'd had male roommates before, although none of them had affected her like Jordan did.

She unlocked the door leading to her room and threw it open so she could make a fast exit.

Then she unlocked Jordan's door, pushed it open a few inches and called through it, "All done. Sorry to bother you," before sprinting for the safety of her bedroom.

Where she would normally have stared at the ceiling the rest of the night, the exhaustion of pregnancy had her dropping off to sleep. She also blamed pregnancy hormones for her vivid dreams of Jordan's touch warming her skin, his mouth making her lips ache, his eyes peering into her soul.

As she awoke the next morning feeling as if she'd crammed four months of catch-up sleep into one night, she attributed that heart-thudding bit of loneliness to pregnancy, too.

She did her best to shrug it all off. All the literature had said to expect exhaustion, mood swings and strange dreams.

A pitter-patter on her door had her trying to push the sleep from her befuddled brain.

A hesitant feminine voice called through the thick wood. "Miss Novak? Are you all right in there?"

"Fine." Her voice came out sleep-roughened and cracked. She cleared her throat. "Just fine."

She didn't sound any finer the second time around.

"Oh. Okay." Youth and uncertainty carried through the door. "Well, if you want me to give you a lift into work…"

Work?

Deseré opened the door about four inches, hanging onto the edge for security. Trying to make sense of this morning, she stuck her head out to see the girl face-to-face, too aware that she hadn't even given her herself a glance yet. "It's Saturday, right?"

The girl's gaze took in Deseré's hair and rumpled scrubs before politely going back to her face. "Yes, ma'am."

Deseré could feel the drying drool in the corner of her mouth as her reasoning skills kicked in. "Um, we have Saturday hours, don't we?"

Sympathy and understanding showed in the girl's tone of voice. "Yes, ma'am."

Deep-breath time. "Give me a few seconds."

In record time Deseré ran a toothbrush across her teeth and a hairbrush across her bride-of-Frankenstein hair.

With only a half second of deliberation, she threw on horribly wrinkled dress pants, leaving the top button undone, a blouse that should be tucked in and looked tacky hanging loose, her sturdy nursing tennis shoes with the laces loosened because her swelling feet couldn't take those filthy, flimsy sandals, and a dusting of face powder and blush with a dash of lipstick because she couldn't stop herself.

Fighting to keep panic from her voice, she threw open her bedroom door and called into the hallway, "Ready."

"Yes, ma'am." The girl waiting in the hallway across from her bedroom door inspected her. "We've got spare scrubs at work if you'd rather."

"That would be nice."

And that was the last opportunity she had to speak before they arrived at the clinic just a few minutes away as she'd had no inclination to shout over the radio playing country music cranked up loud enough to buzz the car's speakers.

The clinic was a sixties-style square box with pink brick and white plastic shutters. Skeletons of dead chrysanthemums spiked up in the untended front flowerbed. Stenciled on the glass of the door were the office hours, including eight till noon Saturdays.

And it was now nine-fifteen. She would start her daily bout of morning sickness in approximately forty-five minutes.

Jordan Hart plastered on his best doctor face as he listened to Mrs. Mabel tell him all about her pie-baking incident while he bandaged her cut thumb.

It was a nick. A butterfly bandage would do.

His mind wandered as he pulled out one drawer and then another, looking for supplies.

He'd once been organized, obsessively. But now he couldn't seem to stay focused long enough to put anything in order, including his own mind.

Everyone he'd talked to, all the counselors they'd set him up with before his discharge, had assured him that re-entry into the calm, sedate civilian world would take a bit of adjustment after being on the front lines for eighteen months.

Okay. He got that. But in the meantime his patients were suffering for his weakness.

Where was that nurse practitioner he'd hired last night?

Jordan drew in a big breath. He knew exactly what had happened. No one had mentioned to her that they kept Saturday hours.

His fault. He was in charge of this clinic and therefore responsible.

Jordan froze. Something felt off. What was it?

The exam room was quiet. Mrs. Mabel had stopped talking.

She was staring at him, expecting—expecting what?

He replayed the last few seconds in his mind.

"I'm sure your pie is worth the effort. A store-bought pie wouldn't be the same." It came out flat and mechanical. But apparently Mabel didn't need enthusiasm as she gave him a wrinkled smile.

"That's what my husband always used to say."

Jordan knew that. Somewhere in his subconscious he'd remembered Mrs. Mabel saying that exact thing about her dearly departed husband of forty-five years, which was why he'd parroted it back to her.

A knock sounded on the exam-room door, a no-nonsense, staccato rap.

He pushed the door open and saw his newest employee standing there. Deseré.

He had an instant collage of images in his brain of her body against his as he held her back from climbing into the arena too soon, of her holding Rusty's head, of her in his shower.

The emotions associated with those memories overshadowed his powers of speech. He'd been putting his feelings in a box for a long time—for years, way before Afghanistan. Way before medical school. Way before adulthood.

After he'd successfully exerted control over them for so many years, why now? Why now did that control elude him so that his emotions could play havoc with his logic?

As memories of seeing her naked kept flashing in his mind, Jordan didn't dare look at her too closely right now.

Last night had almost been his undoing.

And today he was too close to losing his control to risk an in-depth analysis of why the V seemed deeper on her boxy top than on his other employees' tops.

"Are you the new girl I heard about? The one who showed up at the rodeo last night?" Mrs. Mabel asked, looking from him to Deseré and back again.

Deseré as in desire. Yeah, it fit her.

A wedge of reality crowded past the image of her foggy image in the mirror.

Making a half-turn back to Mrs. Mabel, he told her, "This is my new nurse practitioner, Deseré Novak. She'll take good care of you."

He dragged his attention to a point around her right earlobe as he said, "Take over here, Deseré." He sounded gruff, even to his own ears.

He'd never considered scrubs sexy before. But now—now he thought of them as a clever disguise to hide what was underneath.

With a nod of his head he gestured to Mrs. Mabel, who was staring at Deseré.

"Simple cut. A butterfly bandage will do," he said,

to have something to say. A nurse practitioner would know that as well as he did.

She wouldn't know where anything was, but she could do no worse job of this than he was doing. At least Mrs. Mabel's chart was in plain sight on the counter.

Without a glance in Deseré's direction, he walked past her and out the door. Even though he had been overly cautious to not brush against her, he still felt the heat of her body as he walked past.

In fact, he felt that heat all the way down the hallway, even after he'd shut the door to his private office.

Too many thoughts rushed his brain—what little brain he still had functioning. Lust was at the top of the list. Then there was the relief he'd felt last night when he'd been able to walk away from responsibility, dumping it all on Deseré. And guilt for both the dumping of responsibility and for the relief he'd felt about it. Yeah, he was screwed up.

Worry for Rusty, worry about money, worry about the gossip his living arrangements with Deseré would cause—not that he wasn't used to it, but she didn't deserve it—all crowded and swirled around, giving him a headache.

He didn't know what he would do about most of those chaotic thoughts, other than try to ignore them.

Ha! That would be like ignoring a stampede of longhorns barreling down on him.

But ignore them he would. It was the only way to make it through patient rounds.

He clenched his jaw, ignoring the shooting pain arcing through his whole head. No—welcoming the pain because it would help to seal in his intention to ignore anything and everything having to do with Deseré Novak.

Real practical, Hart. She works for you. She sleeps in the bedroom next to yours. How are you going to ignore that?

He could no more ignore Deseré than he could ignore the light but persistent knock on his door.

"Doc Hart?" a small female voice called.

Not Deseré, he was relieved to hear, but Katey, who only spoke in a shy voice barely above a whisper.

He rubbed his hand over his face, trying to erase any signs of turmoil as he moved toward his office door.

"Do you need something, Katey?"

Katey blushed under his direct questioning, even though he'd been sure to keep his tone quiet and calm.

She was as skittish as a wild colt. Not the best quality for a part-time receptionist, but she needed the job and was willing to work a short week in return for work/study credit and a pittance of a paycheck, which was pretty much all he could afford to pay.

Katey looked down at the pink handwritten note in her hand. "Rusty called from the hospital. They set his arm this morning. His concussion is out of the danger range. He's being released later this afternoon and could use a ride home. Could you send Plato?"

"Good news." Very good news. Not only was Rusty doing well, but now he had a reason to stay away from his own house until Deseré had had time to do her bathroom stuff and climb into bed.

Ignoring the image his brain had supplied of her in *his* bed, he deliberately blinked. "Thanks, Katey. Call him back and tell him I'll pick him up."

He stepped back to close his door but Katey took a step forward, stopping him. No small feat for her.

Good for her. Maybe this job was helping her in some small way, just like his sister had hoped it would.

Sissy was good at nudging people into the right places so everyone ended up better for it.

Only with him her nudge had always been more like a shove. He guessed he was just stubborn that way. When he'd been ready to cut the clinic's hours, she'd nagged him ceaselessly until she'd talked him into hiring help instead, even doing all the applicant searches herself.

Jordan was fairly sure Sissy had screwed up this time, though, by pushing Deseré into his path. Deseré didn't deserve to be tarnished by his shortcomings and sins.

Katey gave a nervous squeak and Jordan realized his expression might have turned less than placid.

He kept his voice low and soft, like he was gentling a new foal. "Okay. Anything else?"

Katey dug one toe of her shoe into the worn tile flooring. "You said we could order pizzas on Saturdays if we get the two-for-ones?"

"Sure."

"Pepperoni for me and Nurse Harper. Sausage and onion for you, right, Dr. Hart?"

"Yes, please." He should let it go. It was a little thing and he should let it work itself out but… "Wait. Find out what Ms. Novak likes. I'll eat whatever she chooses."

As long as she didn't choose mushroom. But, then, that would put an end to the fantasy, wouldn't it? What man could fall for a woman who liked mushrooms on her pizza?

Deseré rolled the taste of hot pizza around her mouth, savoring every burst on her tastebuds. Who would have guessed that a town this size would have such great pizza?

The sausage was homemade, Katey had told her. And the mushrooms were fresh and sautéed instead of raw to bring out a more intense flavor.

Utterly delicious. Especially since last night's dinner of chili-covered everything had been too many hours ago to satisfy baby James and he clearly hadn't appreciated the super-sugary cinnamon rolls Katey had fetched when she'd found out Deseré hadn't had breakfast.

Deseré's standard ten o'clock stomach flip had confirmed baby James's opinion of her food choice—not that she'd really had a choice.

Free food, baby. We don't turn down food. Then she promised, *It won't always be this way,* determined to sound confident even in her private thoughts. Who knew what babies picked up?

A shifting movement from her dining partner reminded her that reticent doctors could pick up plenty, so she quickly smoothed out any expression she might have inadvertently been showing.

Just as the man across from her was doing.

Apparently, Dr. Hart was also a picky eater.

He sat across from her in the minuscule staff break room, and carefully used his fork to remove the offending fungi, making sure the little gray bits didn't touch his fingers.

Dr. Hart. After he'd done the arrogant doctor stereotype thing and abandoned her to muddle through the rest of the morning exams on her own, she'd been able to think of him as Dr. Hart all morning long, instead of the Jordan of her dreams.

But now, with his hair falling into his eyes as he picked his way through another piece of pizza, he was fast becoming Jordan again.

"I'm sure Nancy and Katey would have saved you

some of their pizza if you'd asked them to." Although the way those two had almost inhaled their lunch earlier made her statement more doubtful supposition than solid reality.

He shrugged, not bothering to answer her.

The silence made eating uncomfortable as he totally ignored her. It also challenged her.

"Mrs. Mabel promised to bring by a pie. I guess you're saving room for it, huh?" Inane conversation was better than no conversation.

He looked up from under his lashes, giving her a look as if she was interrupting an intricate surgical procedure. "Hmm."

Okay, so much for polite small talk.

"I owe a great deal of thanks to Nancy for helping me get acquainted with the clinic's normal operating procedures today. I learned by doing."

He swallowed, as if he'd just forced down one of the innocent mushrooms he found so offensive.

"You did fine." That he'd had to force the compliment out was evident in his brusque delivery.

He looked away toward the corner of the room then back at her again. "Because you were here, we're getting out of the office on time. Usually, I'd still have patients in the waiting room and I'd be here until after six."

As if stringing all those words together at once made him restless, he pushed back from the table and stood. "You can leave whenever you're done here. I'll lock up."

"Wait."

"Oh, Katey picked you up. You need a ride back to the house?"

"No, I can walk it."

"There's not enough shoulder on the road for that

and the ditches are steep. Even though it's close, I'd rather drive you."

Not only did his words sound protective, so did his tone—and his eyes.

A comforting warmth crept up from deep inside her, but it suddenly became uncomfortable. She could take care of herself.

This sensation felt—what did it feel like? She searched through words like suffocating and overbearing. No. None of those.

It felt—nice. "Thanks."

But then he frowned at her, erasing all the good will he'd gained. "About last night…"

Again he looked toward the corner of the room for his words. Very deliberately, he looked back at her, meeting her eyes.

His intensity had her looking away. She ended up focusing on his mouth, instead of those deep, dark eyes of his. His lips revealed a lot more emotion than his eyes did anyway.

"Yes?" she prompted.

"I'm…" He glanced down, breaking contact momentarily before he looked back up and pinned her again. "I'm sorry for walking in on you. I didn't realize… And for forgetting to unlock the door, too. My sister hasn't lived there in a while and I'm not used to sharing…."

His voice sounded like he was being sliced with razorblades, so raw she had to put an end to his pain.

"It's okay. Just a simple mistake." She drew attention to her own mistake to try to ease things. "Like me missing Saturday office hours."

She bit her bottom lip, thinking he had no sense of humor, but she was going for it anyway. "No Sunday hours, right?"

His lips loosened up the slightest bit at the corners, knocking a good half-decade off his age and making the whole room feel easier. "No Sunday hours. My mistake on the weekend mix-up, too."

His mouth, that subtly expressive mouth, relinquished the slightest of quirks at the corners. But Deseré sensed self-deprecating irony more than good humor. Still, it was an improvement of sorts.

"Forgiven." It was one of those words she always wanted to hear but could rarely say herself. But with this man across from her, this stranger who seemed so hard-shelled except for the smallest of tell-tale slips that she was probably imagining, it was easy to say.

"All forgiven," she said, as much for herself as for him, to see how it felt the second time around.

Did she imagine his jaw loosening or was that a trick of the dust dancing on the sunlight as the rays shone through the ancient metal venetian blinds?

Baby James kicked, reminding her of her priorities.

What did it matter, really, how Jordan Hart reacted to her? Except in a professional sense, of course. She had to make herself so valuable he'd keep her, even when he found out about baby James.

"I'll help you close up. I need to know how. Show me what you do."

Jordan hesitated, then nodded. "Okay. We'll start with double-checking the locks on the drug safes."

As he led her through the building, he instructed her to throw all the locks, especially the double bolts on the rear door, to turn on the answering-machine and forward the emergency number to the fire department as the more rural areas didn't have the 911 facility yet and to turn down the thermostat.

As he held the front door open for her——his gentleman gene wouldn't have let him do otherwise—he cleared his throat. "Let's drive you home."

She walked toward where he pointed at his truck in the far corner of the parking lot.

He opened the unlocked passenger door of his truck and held out his hand to help her make the big step from ground to truck cab.

Bracing herself for that moment of contact that should be so impersonal but wouldn't be after the dreams she'd had last night, she put her hand in his.

His strength practically lifted her up and into the truck.

His touch practically burned from her palm into her core.

"Thanks." Hoping he would attribute her breathlessness to the way she had to twist to fasten her seat belt, she covertly rubbed her arm to stop the tingling. The rubbing didn't help.

Maybe scrubbing would.

Which brought her thoughts back to the shower they hadn't shared last night.

Dear heavens, what was happening to her? Why couldn't she keep her wayward thoughts under control?

Before Jordan put the truck into gear, he looked over at her, his expression blank.

"Deseré."

Her name sounded so sexy coming from his mouth. He'd said it soft and low, as if he was afraid of startling her. With just the smallest amount of imagination, she could imagine him whispering like that in her ear.

Pregnant, Deseré, she reminded herself. *You're pregnant. Which means unavailable. So curb the S-E-X contemplations.*

She couldn't look at him. Not right now. Not until she got her hormone-fueled libido under control.

Instead, she turned to look out the side window. The lighting and angle were perfect for catching his reflection there. She'd run out of willpower to look away.

Clearing her throat, she answered, "Yes?"

Motionless, accept for the muscles in his jaw that stood out, clenching and clenching, he stared at her. The air became heavier and heavier with tension.

Deseré would have broken the silence if she could have, but she had no words. And there were times when guttural moans just wouldn't do.

Finally he blew out a breath and his muscles twitched into resignation. "We have to talk."

CHAPTER SIX

WE HAVE TO TALK.

There went all thoughts of sex. Well, most of them anyway.

"Okay." She turned to face him, needing to read more of his body language than the window reflection allowed.

This didn't mean Jordan was firing her, did it? After her first day?

She had worked hard. Had thought quickly on her feet. Had been competent under less than ideal conditions.

Or was it something else? A hundred possible conversations floated through her head, none of them bringing a smile to her face.

But she plastered on a smile anyway, hoping she could defuse whatever situation was about to unfold. "We need to talk? That's usually my line."

He didn't crack the slightest of grins. Didn't loosen the tightness of his shoulders or jaw. Didn't even glance in her direction. Just stared straight ahead through the windshield, his hands loosely crossed and resting on the steering wheel.

The pose was deceptively relaxed. But Deseré had had to read too many men in her life to fall for it.

"You know—" she forced a strained laugh "—it's usually the woman who wants to talk."

No softening on his face, not even a token to be polite. If anything, he seemed to tense more.

She wouldn't go down without a fight. "I'm really sorry about being late today. I didn't know. But it will never happen again, I promise. And I learned a lot about how your office runs. I really like the laid-back family atmosphere and your processes are simple but thorough. Nancy and Katey and I worked really well together, I think."

"You did fine." His fingers were white-knuckled on the steering-wheel. "You did better than fine."

Relief had her sagging back against the seat. "Good. I'm glad you were pleased."

To her own ears, she sounded so polite. So stiff and formal. So puzzled.

Surely he couldn't miss her confusion. Did he like playing games? He hadn't seemed that type. But, then, she wasn't the type most people thought she was, either.

Another reminder that she really didn't know this man.

Suddenly, the truck seemed way too small. And she was sleeping in the same house with him.

Without realizing until she'd done it, she touched the doorhandle, reassuring herself.

He flexed his fingers, leaving them propped loosely once again.

"People will talk." He turned to look at her, leaning back himself, but not in a smooth, relaxed kind of way. More like he was putting space between them.

Then he turned and pinned her, his focus so intense she wanted to look away.

Why had this just become a contest of wills?

Words, she wanted to say. *Use words.*

But obviously he was one of those stoic types.

She made herself hold her ground. It was a pride thing, without reason but so very important to her.

"These *people*. What will they say?"

"They'll say things about you living with me. Not only is this an old-fashioned kind of town, but I'm not their favorite native son." He broke his stare by rubbing a hand across his face. "I had intended to cover all this in the interview and give you a chance to back out gracefully. Sissy, the woman who dropped you off at the house last night, says she didn't bother to mention to you that we would be living there—uh—unchaperoned."

No, he was not going to fire her because of what people might say. No way. No how. "Unchaperoned? That's a rather odd word for two people who are well into adulthood."

Again, he stared out the window. "I don't have the money to pay you more. And, if there is a place that comes open for rent in town, they'll want more than you can afford."

She nodded her understanding. "Nancy told me you've only been back from Afghanistan five weeks."

"Eight." A muscle in his jaw jumped. "I've been back eight weeks. But I've only recently reopened the clinic. It never made much before, but…"

"But?" she encouraged.

But he'd borrowed as much as he could to get it going again. He'd put up the house and the ranch as collateral. And the banker, an old friend of his father's, had given him more than either of the deflated properties were worth.

"You did fine today. Better than fine." He repeated what he'd said earlier. "But I can't ask you to stay."

She realized she'd been clenching her own fingers as she untangled them. Blood rushed to her fingertips, making them tingle with pain. The pain was good. It helped keep the panic at bay.

"We can make this work."

He shook his head. "I can't ask you to—"

"I need this job," she interrupted. "I need this job," she said again, as if repeating herself would make him understand.

He gave her his attention. This time, though, a glimmer of something soft showed in his eyes. Was he giving her a chance? Was she reading hope there as a reflection of her own attitude?

Lifting her chin, she put strength into her voice. "I've got a really thick skin and I've never cared much what people said about me."

Jordan studied the woman who sat as far from him as the truck seat would permit. Her eyes said it all. Determination. Bravado. Desperation.

And a glint that warned anyone and everyone who stood in her way that they wouldn't have an easy time of it.

"Neither have I." He put behind him all the gossip they would have to endure. All the censure. The possible loss of business because Jordan Hart was up to his wild ways again.

No, he didn't put it behind him. He welcomed it. *Judge me? Bring it on.*

He was at his best when he was fighting the status quo. That's how he had survived his childhood and teenage years. That's how he would survive now.

And for the second time in two days this woman had brought life to the soul he'd thought had died within his body.

* * *

That was all the talking Jordan did voluntarily as they drove toward his house—now her home, too. But his silence wasn't awkward at all. In fact, it was rather comforting. The radio played in the background, softening the air.

Deseré felt her shoulders start to relax, not realizing until now that she'd had them hunched so defensively.

This might be the first time since she'd shoved all her belongings into her car that she felt she could let down her guard.

Santone might come after her, as he'd threatened to, but the man sitting next to her would never let Santone harm her. She knew that as well as she knew the sun would set in the west this evening.

Jordon broke into her contemplations. "I've got to run by the post office and pick up the mail."

"Okay." No mail delivery meant one step farther away from her sister's husband being able to track her down.

A quick stop, a handful of envelopes and circulars, most of which got dumped in the trash can outside the post office, and they were on their way again.

As they wove in and out of the narrow asphalt streets, Deseré paid better attention to landmarks and street names than she had when Katey had driven her to the clinic. Judging by the architecture, the small town seemed to have had two growth spurts, once in the nineteen-twenties and again in the nineteen-sixties.

"The town's been around awhile, huh?"

"Uh-huh."

"Nancy said your dad live in Dallas now."

"Uh-huh."

Nancy hadn't said why his dad no longer lived there,

but there was an air of taboo about Jordan's brief answers.

Jordan was definitely the strong, silent type.

Nancy had said he'd always been quiet. She'd hinted at some teenage tragedy that had made him remote. Or made the town remote from him.

Whatever the town was holding against him—and didn't they all have teenage moments they'd rather forget—? Deseré was certain they were wrong. Her ability to read people had never been so far off that she had totally misjudged someone.

Since the conversation had been in whispered snatches, Deseré wasn't quite sure about the whole story. But she'd rather hear it from Jordan than from gossip. If she needed to hear it at all.

"Have you always lived in Piney Woods?"

He let out a breath at her question. For a moment she thought he wouldn't answer. "Until high school graduation when I joined the army. Then there was college while I was in the reserves."

Turning onto the street that led to Jordan's home, she saw huge front yards mostly landscaped with mature oak and pecan trees and drought-tolerant evergreen bushes.

"Nancy said you were in Afghanistan. How long?"

"Three tours of duty."

"I hear things got pretty rough over there."

He shrugged, the casual gesture marred by the tenseness in his jaw. "I had a job to do. I did it."

Obviously, not a place he wanted to go. Deseré wasn't sure why she'd tried to lead him there.

She'd just as soon not tell Jordan her own life story. She understood privacy. Exposure led to vulnerability. And vulnerability led to pain.

Trying to get back to a neutral, impersonal place, she said, "I bet you're glad to be home, huh?"

Jordan slowed to a crawl to turn into the driveway. "It needs work."

From what Deseré had seen, the Hart house was one of the largest in town but not the best cared for. The deep covered porch needed a good sweeping to clear the dust and cobwebs. It could use a couple of lawn chairs or, better yet, a couple of rockers to make it look inviting. Maybe a few flowering plants, too.

But, then, it wasn't really her home, was it? Just a place to stay for however long she could manage it.

Jordan stopped short of the garage where she had parked so haphazardly last night, quickly climbed out of the truck and opened her door as she was still unbuckling her seat belt and gathering her purse.

He held out his hand and she took it—and barely kept herself from jerking back when their palms touched, creating a tingle that reached from her fingertips to her heart.

Which must be the pregnancy hormones talking, of course. The same hormones that were insisting she needed a nap as soon as possible.

But sleeping in the house with the man who made her tingle didn't give her a warm, cozy feeling. In fact, it gave her the exact opposite, where beds were desired but sleeping was optional.

She was an idiot. If she had any sense at all, she would be wary, afraid even. But her good sense failed her.

And now, seconds too late, she realized she was still holding Jordan's hand.

"You okay?" His drawl made his deep voice sound richer than cane syrup.

"Fine." She rubbed her hand on her pants leg. "Just tired."

She hadn't meant to admit that. Hadn't meant to show any weakness. Hadn't meant to hold onto his hand, either.

But she was too tired to do anything but tell the truth.

He nodded, accepting her explanation without question.

"I'm going to run in for a few minutes and pack enough to keep me overnight. I'll spend it out at the ranch and give you the house to yourself. The pantry and refrigerator are stocked fairly well. Help yourself."

Nancy had told her about the family ranch, the one Jordan had refused to take over from his father, choosing the army instead. It existed as a scaled-back version of its former self, as they bred cutting horses instead of the hundreds of head of cattle they had once raised. It produced only enough income for his foreman, his cousin Rusty, with the help of one aging cowboy, the one she'd met last night that everyone called Plato.

She wanted to ask how he could trust her to turn over his house to her without even knowing her. She would have never trusted a stranger like this.

Instead, she said, "I thought we talked about not worrying about town gossip. You really don't have to be so noble."

He shook his head. "Don't paint me as something I'm not. Being noble isn't what this is about."

Then what is this about? She wanted to ask what she should do if she heard things go bump in the middle of the night—not that she'd ever needed a man around for that. In fact, it was usually a man wanting to go bump that she did her best to avoid. But Jordan made her feel—protected? Respected? Safe?

How could that be? She'd only met him yesterday. Pregnancy hormones, right? But even to herself that explanation was running thin.

"I don't want to push you out of your own home."

"You're not pushing me anywhere." He tightened his lips as if he was trying to keep the words in. Finally, he said, "With Rusty out of commission, I need to pick up his slack at the ranch. There's no sense in driving out there, getting in a few hours then driving back, when I can stay the night and use those extra hours to get some work in."

That made sense. But…

She wanted to ask him to stay, and she had no idea why.

So all she said was, "Okay."

He paused as if waiting for more. But when no more was forthcoming, he nodded and said, "Okay," too.

And five minutes later, while she sequestered herself in her room, listening for him to leave, she heard the front door close and his truck drive off.

And she was so overcome with—well, with everything that exhaustion struck her and she fell into bed and slept a solid ten hours.

Jordan drove away, resisting looking in the rear-view mirror. *Don't look back.* It's something he'd tried to learn, but so far hadn't been very successful.

No, she wasn't standing on the porch, watching him drive away. Why did that disappoint him?

Why did he feel lonely and alone when all these weeks he'd felt nothing but numb?

Why did he think it had something to do with Deseré Novak?

And what was he going to do about it?

Nothing. Absolutely nothing.

He spent all his next waking hours mending fences, hauling hay and throwing himself into whatever hard labor he could find to make himself think about nothing. Absolutely nothing but the work in front of him.

If he could only control his sleeping hours as well.

After waking up and fixing a middle-of-the-night snack of scrambled eggs, Deseré went back to bed and slept until midmorning.

And that's how her weekend went. Eat, sleep, do a load of laundry and take another nap.

By Monday morning she felt better rested than she had felt in years.

And she made it to the office early, ready to begin her new life, realizing she felt happier than she'd felt in years, too.

If only she could see further into the future than today, her life would be perfect.

But for now one day at a time was enough.

Jordan Hart was one unhappy man.

Sleeping on a cot in the tack room of the barn might have been fun when he was in his pre-teens, but that flimsy twenty-year-old rack of metal and saggy canvas didn't offer much comfort to his used and abused adult body.

Used. His thoughts went back to the dreams that had kept him on edge as much as the rickety cot had.

The sound of a truck pulling up outside the barn made Jordan push himself off the cot, stretching and moaning as he tried to loosen up the tight muscles making his back and ribs scream.

He'd just shaken out the boots he'd taken off the night

before and was stamping onto his feet when he heard Rusty call out, "Hey, Jordan, is that you in there?"

"Yes, Rusty, it's me."

Rusty leaned against the door frame. The thick linen canvas of his sling draped across his chest kept his arm immobile. "Plato said you were out here early. I didn't realize that meant you slept out here, too."

"Easier to get an early start this way."

"So you just left that little nurse to herself in your house?"

"Nurse practitioner. And, yes, she's a grown woman. She can take care of herself."

"That's not really what I was talking about. What if she strips your house and drives off with all your stuff?"

"Then I'll have less stuff I have to clean and dust, won't I?" But Jordan couldn't leave it there. For some reason he had to go one step further and defend her. "Deseré's not like that."

"Deseré. Pretty sexy name, huh?" Rusty grinned. "Just what is she like?"

Jordan glared at Rusty with enough fierceness to wipe the grin off Rusty's face. "She's a good enough nurse practitioner to take care of you when you're unconscious, facedown in the dirt."

Rusty backed off. "If you trust her, I trust her."

Trust. That word made him uncomfortable. "It's not a matter of trust. Letting her live in the house is a matter of necessity."

"Necessity is getting Madonna groomed for the possible buyer coming in this afternoon."

Jordan nodded in agreement. He deeply regretted needing to sell the brood mare, but she wasn't in foal and he couldn't afford to keep feeding her over the winter if she wasn't going to produce offspring that he could sell in the spring.

While Rusty awkwardly reached for the curry brush and other grooming equipment single-handedly, Jordan turned away from his cousin to fold up the blanket and cot he'd used.

Rusty knew the financial difficulties Jordan was going through. They had talked about it when Jordan had reopened the clinic. Rusty and Plato had both agreed to work only part-time at the ranch and to make the difference up helping out on neighboring ranches. Which meant that Jordan had needed to spend more hours at the ranch even before Rusty had injured himself.

But those hours wouldn't include sleeping in the tack room again. He'd tortured his body to put some mind-clearing distance between himself and Deseré Novak, only to have her inside his head the moment he'd fallen asleep.

Deseré. Yes, it was a sexy name. And she had a sexy body to go with it.

He'd dreamed of her all night long.

Anyone would think that the hard, sweaty, muscle-wrecking job of making hay from sunup to past sundown all day yesterday would have meant he had a dreamless sleep last night.

Not so.

But he hadn't had nightmares. Far from it. The only thing disturbing about the dreams he'd had was the frustration of waking up alone.

Rusty stopped on his way out of the tack room. "You know, Jordan, it's been a long time since I've seen you smile."

He groaned and wiped his hand over his face, too

aware of his wry grin as he thought about those wonderfully provocative nocturnal fantasies he'd enjoyed.

How long had it been since he'd actually woken up happy?

Before he could come up with an explanation, Rusty punched him in the shoulder. "If Deseré Novak is responsible, I might just be in love with the woman."

Irrational jealousy forced a growl from Jordan's throat. Deseré was his—at least, in his dreams.

Thankfully, Rusty left the tack room before Jordan had to explain his caveman growl.

But the futility of turning that fantasy into reality had made his attitude plummet.

As he drove back into town to catch a shower before going into the clinic, he attempted to rationalize his thoughts about the drastic mood swings he owed to a woman he'd only met a few days ago, a woman he employed.

A woman who shared his responsibilities, lightening his load, providing him with a safety net for when his head wasn't in the game.

A woman he hardly knew.

A woman who had already vacated his house and left for her day at the clinic by the time he pulled up in his driveway.

His head was throbbing by the time he climbed from his truck. He needed aspirin and a shower, in that order.

With Deseré gone, he could catch a private moment of peace. Well, as much peace as his overactive imagination would allow him anyway. Although the bathroom they shared was spotless, Deseré's scent lingered in the air.

During his icy shower Jordan deliberately concentrated on the work that needed to be done on the ranch.

With Rusty's arm broken, a lot of the physical labor would fall on Plato, but the man was in his seventies. Jordan would make a point of going out there more often.

If Deseré settled in the way he thought she would, he would have more free time away from the office, which would be good for everyone.

But what was he going to do about his fascination with her?

He'd always been a man who preferred to face problems straight on. But how prudent was telling the woman who now lived in his house that he dreamed of her?

Deseré had got in to the clinic an hour early. If anyone asked, she would truthfully tell them she wanted to review charts for the patients coming in today. Her nature was to be thorough. Working in this small clinic would let her indulge in that thoroughness, unlike the walk-in clinic she'd worked at in New Orleans.

But the real reason was that the house was filled with Jordan, even though he hadn't been there all weekend. She saw him in the jeans and shirts hanging in the laundry room. She smelled him in the scent of his detergent. She heard him in the songs on the radio, tuned to the same channel as in his truck.

And she felt him in her dreams, as if he were right beside her, running his hand down her spine, breathing in her ear. Whispering words of love and assurance.

While love at first sight might be a myth, lust at first sight certainly wasn't.

Playing it safe, ignoring her fascination with him, pretending it didn't exist was the prudent thing to do. But Deseré had always taken problems on straight on.

Letting them build until they were too big to handle wasn't her way.

She needed this job. Would being forthright about her attraction to Jordan put it in jeopardy?

And how would they live together amicably and platonically afterward?

It wasn't like her enthrallment with Jordan was going to go anywhere. It was all fantasy in her own head with not a shred of reality about it.

She bit her lip, agonizing over her indecision.

Play it safe, Deseré. That's what her sister would tell her.

But she wasn't Celeste. And Jordan definitely wasn't Santone.

For which Deseré was very grateful.

"Good morning, Dr. Hart," said Deseré as Jordan twisted his key and pushed the self-locking door open.

From over the top of the computer monitor she shot him a bright smile.

He had remembered that she was on the high end of the pretty scale, but that smile turned her into a radiant beauty.

He swallowed down his reaction and answered evenly, "Good morning. Busy schedule today?"

"Looks like it. No open time slots but they aren't all doubles, so we will have a few minutes every now and then."

"I wouldn't count on that. We have more walk-ins than appointments." He should be glad about the heavy schedule and the revenue it would bring in. Instead, he was worried about the focus he would need to keep his head in the game, patient after patient.

But, then, he no longer carried the full load himself, did he? All because of her.

He took a step toward Deseré, to look over her shoulder, to surreptitiously smell her hair. To find a reason to brush against her. To see if that blood-rushing excitement when they touched had only been in his imagination.

A knock on the glass office door interrupted that little trip down fantasy lane. Taking his attention away from this woman who would be on her way to something bigger and better as soon as she exorcised whatever demons she was running from, if she had any smarts at all.

And Jordan had seen evidence that she was very, very smart.

"Dr. Hart? Dr. Hart?" Mrs. Mabel had her face pressed against the glass, the better to look in and see what was happening beyond that locked door.

Jordan didn't know if he was more exasperated or relieved that Mrs. Mabel was interrupting these moments alone with Deseré. He wasn't sure about most things when it came to his new nurse practitioner.

Mrs. Mabel came in with a pie carrier in one hand and a clear plastic freezer bag in the other.

"Fresh, just out of the oven," she said by way of greeting. The odor of burnt pie crust filled the air as she lifted the cover.

"Lovely," Deseré murmured as she reached for the pie.

But Mabel held tight. Giving Jordan a once-over, she turned her full attention to Deseré.

"How did you find Dr. Hart's home, dear? It was quite the showplace back when it was built. Such a shame, though, that Dr. Hart had to be displaced. I'm sure those old bunks at your father's ranch aren't nearly as comfortable. And such a long drive back and forth every day.

"But, then, it wouldn't do at all for the two of you to stay in the same house, now, would it? Your momma would roll over in her grave if she thought the two of you were staying in the same house all by yourselves. So, of course, when someone from my Sunday School class, and I won't say who because we don't tell tales, now, do we, said she thought you both slept there Friday night, I told her I'd met you and you were a nice girl and she must be mistaken. Right, dear?"

Jordan hoped he would never be the recipient of the cold smile Deseré gave Mabel. Tightly, she asked, "Would you like me to take that pie to our break room?"

Jordan admired her restraint. He also wasn't sure what to do or say next. If it were only him, he'd let Mrs. Mabel know she had overstepped the mark. But that would be confirming the rumors, wouldn't it? And that didn't seem to be the gentlemanly thing to do. But neither did it sit well with him to let Mabel's nosey comments go unrebuked.

"Of course, dear. I have something a bit delicate to ask Dr. Hart and this will give us a chance to chat."

Jordan narrowed his eyes. "Do we need to step into an examination room? If so, I can check the schedule and work you in, but it may be a while."

At the mention of being alone with Jordan in an exam room Mabel's eyes lit up. But when he said she'd have to wait her turn, that light died a quick death.

"No need for that," she said. She held up the plastic bag. "I need to know what this is."

Inside was a used pregnancy test. Mabel was at least two decades past her childbearing years.

"And why do you need to know that?" His tone was low and quiet. Anyone who knew him well knew to back off immediately.

But Mrs. Mabel didn't know him well at all.

Instead, she pressed on. "I found it in my niece's bathroom trashcan. She's staying with me, you know? Such a handful."

Her niece, *the handful*, had recently returned to Piney Woods after her cheating husband had left her. She was working at a church daycare during the day and the local diner at night, trying to get back on her feet. Jordan knew all this because she'd come in to request an STD test just to be sure she was okay.

"I suggest you stop dealing in trash." Jordan drew himself up to his full height and glared down at Mabel, making his meaning crystal clear. He took the plastic bag from her and walked to the door, holding it open. "Next time, make an appointment."

From behind him, Deseré cleared her throat. "Oh, and, Mrs. Mabel, not only are Jordan and I sharing a house, we also shared a shower."

The second the door closed behind Mrs. Mabel, Deseré clasped her hand over her mouth. "I am *so* sorry," filtered through her fingers loud and clear.

And Jordan laughed—a real, honest-to-goodness, joyous laugh.

"I'm not," he answered her, laughing again just because he could. When had he last felt this light? This unrestricted? Ever?

With that laugh, it felt like he released a lifetime of anxiety.

Still mortified, Deseré uncovered her mouth but bit her bottom lip.

"Don't." He had the strongest desire to kiss that lip free.

What was it about this woman that entranced him?

This was so unlike him. What was wrong with him?

And why did it feel so right?

It had been so long since he'd felt anything for anyone but this wasn't just anyone.

The urge was so strong to touch her that he reached out and brushed a strand of hair from her cheek.

His fingertips tingled, wanting more.

Her indrawn breath told him she'd been affected, too.

But how had he affected her?

He struggled to think rationally, to read her downcast eyes, to interpret the brace of her shoulders. To determine if she had really leaned into him or if it was purely his wishful thinking.

He shifted on his feet, subtly putting distance between them. What had he just done?

This was the woman he worked with. The woman he employed. The woman who lived in his house and *whom he had seen naked in his shower*.

Now was not the time to be thinking of that.

Shreds of professionalism as well as practicality wrapped around him, reining him in.

Deseré wasn't a one-night stand.

She could not be trifled with.

Not that he would do that. He had too much respect for her.

Immediately he lowered his hand to his side and took a step back. "Now it's my turn to say I'm sorry."

Catching her lip again, but this time with a sparkle in her eye, she looked at him. "I'm not."

Her admission changed everything, turning their relationship from purely professional into the possibility of more.

Under his intense study she glowed a beautiful shade of pink.

"I've never known a woman who blushed before."

With color still high in her cheeks, she took a deep breath. "This isn't normal for me. I don't usually—"

Trying to smooth over the awkwardness, he interrupted with, "We're both adults—" until she held up her hand.

"I'd like to clear the air here, please."

"Okay." He crossed his arms to keep from reaching for her again.

"This is—what I'm feeling is—" She took a breath, her eyes begging him to understand. "Not real."

He raised one eyebrow. "Not real? It feels pretty real to me."

Deseré took another deep breath. "Maybe you had better tell me what you're feeling, then." Because she knew he couldn't be feeling what she was feeling.

His jaw worked, like he was mulling over a particularly difficult problem. Blowing out a breath, he nodded, apparently coming to a decision.

"Attraction?" Looking away from her, not meeting her eyes. "Insanity?" He answered as questions, giving her room to confirm or deny them.

"Attraction," she confirmed, relieved to have it out in the open. Her practical nature couldn't let her leave it at that. "But we don't really know each other. And we are living in the same house. So maybe we'd better not act on it, okay?"

Watching him closely, Deseré identified regret, loss

and relief among all the myriad emotions that crossed through his eyes.

And then there was that gut-wrenching blankness as his eyes lost their luster and turned flat and unreadable.

With his face as still and solemn as the night he'd opened his bedroom door to her, he said, "Okay. Yeah. That was a mistake."

His eyes left her feeling cold and lonely. What could she do? What could she say to warm those eyes again?

She cleared her throat, swallowing past the caution Celeste would have advised. "How about growing friendship? We could do that, couldn't we?"

A faint spark flickered in his eyes. "Maybe."

She couldn't resist. She reached toward him to—

She would never know what she would have done because Nancy rapped on the door, calling loud enough for them to hear her. "Hey, can you unlock this? I gave Deseré my key and haven't made a new one yet."

How long had she been out there? What had she heard? What did it matter, with the story Mrs. Mabel was surely spreading far and wide?

As if Jordan had exactly the same thought, he turned a searching gaze on her, capturing her total focus. "About Mrs. Mabel. Chin high has always worked the best for me."

"Chin high—" she lifted hers a few millimeters "—has always worked for me, too."

As if that moment of shared pasts knocked down a few of the bricks between them, Jordan's eyes deepened so that a glimmer of his former laughing self showed through.

And with that he turned and unlocked the door and they began their day.

* * *

Jordan found enough to do to keep himself busy as Deseré finished her charting duties. A stickler for precise charting, he'd been relieved to find that Deseré was as thorough as he could have asked for.

In fact, she was thorough and competent all round. Saturday's office hours hadn't been a fluke.

For the first time since he'd returned, Jordan didn't feel drained at the end of the workday.

Plastering on his best meet-the-patient face hadn't taken as much out of him as usual, especially when he'd given the more trying patients to Deseré.

And she carried her load, seeing almost as many patients as he had. She had the knack of being able to engage in conversation enough to make the patient comfortable yet not spend too long with one patient at another patient's expense.

And she hadn't seemed to mind the chatty ones at all. She was a good listener, able to pick out enough clues from the prattle of Mr. Grayson to figure out he hadn't been taking his insulin consistently. Figuring out Tina's stomachache was due to a math test she hadn't studied for, instead of some rare and mysterious ailment that made her roll her eyes dramatically while pressing her fist into her belly.

Listening compassionately to Mrs. Mabel's niece talk about options for her pregnancy, even though they didn't handle obstetrics in their office and Deseré had already given the girl the names of several obstetricians to see in Longview.

His day had been unstressed, with a few football physicals, a sinus infection, two head colds and a case of colic that had made the whole office wince in sympathy.

He realized he was staring at her when she looked

up from filing the last chart and asked, "You're waiting on me, aren't you? I think I've got the closing procedure down, but you might want to check me on it."

He gave her a shrug, not really knowing why he was waiting for her but willing to use her explanation instead of telling her the truth, that he felt good in her company and it was a feeling he wanted to hang onto as long as it lasted.

As with everything else she'd done that day, she closed up thoroughly and efficiently, ignoring him as she went through the checklist.

As she turned the last key in the last lock, he touched her arm to claim her attention.

Worry crinkled the corners of her eyes. "Did I forget something?"

"No, you didn't forget anything."

"I told you I was good at what I did." She gave him one of those life-affirming smiles with a side order of self-confidence. The combination made him want to do more than touch her. He wanted to put his lips on that smile and draw it in to become a part of him.

He wanted to be a part of her, too.

For a man who had always wanted to live his life alone, the sensation made him feel too hemmed in.

Plato had said he'd known, the moment he'd laid eyes on his wife, that she was the one. Now, fifty-three years later, she still made his heart race.

Jordan's heart was racing. Did that mean—?

No, those things only happened in movies and romance novels. Lust at first sight? Sure. But the other thing? No. No way.

He took a step away, noting the swing of her hair as she shifted her purse onto her shoulder. That oversize bag was an excellent barrier, intended or not. He took another step back, putting more space between them.

That's it. Keep the attraction at arm's length.

"We're out of milk. I need to stop by the grocery store. Since your compensation comes with room and board, you could come with me and pick up whatever you want to stock the refrigerator and pantry with. We can swing by here afterward and pick up your car."

Darkness crossed Deseré's bright eyes, but she blinked it away.

"That sounds wonderful." Her voice was far more enthusiastic than a simple trip to the grocery store warranted.

They were just groceries. What gave him the suspicion she'd gone hungry before?

Never again. Not under his watch.

"I'll add you to my account while we're there so you can buy whatever you need whenever you need it."

She nodded, acknowledging without replying except for the hope and gratitude her eyes reflected, making him feel like some kind of superhero.

He held the clinic door open for her then gave it a good jerk behind him to make sure it had locked when it closed. She was a couple of paces in front of him and as Jordan followed Deseré out to his truck, he tried to look anywhere but at her sassy bottom.

But he failed.

Don't think about her. Don't think about that almost-kiss. Don't think about wanting to take it all the way. Don't think.

Yeah, not thinking would not be a good thing. That would mean he'd let his body take over, do its own thing, and frankly, after her big statement about not wanting to do anything about their attraction, that would be a mistake.

Because his body wanted her. And hers wanted his. But there were too many reasons why that would be a bad thing, not least that his head wasn't in the right place for a relationship.

Taking two big steps forward, he reached the passenger door, unlocked it and opened it. Not thinking, he reached for her elbow to help her in. A thrill went through him so strongly it made him shake in his boots.

Not thinking.

Not thinking, he dropped her elbow and she had to grab the doorhandle to keep her balance.

"Sorry," he muttered, his voice raw from the strain of keeping his hands to himself.

"No biggie," she murmured back, sounding raspy. What would she sound like after a hard night in his bed, screaming his name?

How could one innocent touch make him come so alive?

And why was he so reluctant to sink back into that safe numb state he'd been in before she'd shown up at the rodeo arena?

Once he was securely belted into his own seat, he forced himself to think.

This was about sex. Pure and simple. It had been a while—a long while.

He should look up old friends. Make a few calls. Plan to go out of town for the weekend.

The ragged-edged psychologist's card he'd carried in his wallet ever since he'd been discharged felt heavy. Urgent, even.

As if Deseré could overhear his thoughts—as if it would make a difference if she could—he fiddled with the volume on the radio, turning it loud enough to make talking inconvenient.

Raising his voice, he asked, "Is this okay?"

She nodded her head, not bothering to answer.

Maybe that was for the best. Right now, her voice was beginning to cause as much reaction in him as her touch did.

He took a deep breath, and realized her scent did the same.

The cab of his truck had never seemed so small and his need for a woman had never seemed so large.

As he put the truck in gear, he admitted to himself that not just any woman would do.

Deseré. She was the only one he wanted.

And she had said it wasn't real.

CHAPTER SEVEN

As the next few days turned into weeks, Deseré and Jordan fell into an easy working relationship.

So Deseré's world was half-good. If only their personal relationship was as easy.

But personal experience had taught her that half-good was better than no good.

The gossip going around in town seemed to increase business instead of diminish it. Everyone was grateful to have medical facilities operating in Piney Woods so they only whispered behind her back. And some of the town's people had even gone out of their way to be friendly. Deseré suspected she had Nancy with her strong community ties to thank for that. And maybe the town wasn't as strongly against Jordan as they once had been, or as he'd thought they were.

She rubbed her belly, feeling the weight of baby James as she felt the weight on her mind. How hard was it to say, "Jordan, I'm pregnant."?

How hard was it to talk about her sister? To say aloud how alone she felt? To give voice to all her uncertainties and fears?

No. Easier to swallow all that down.

Time would make the telling unavoidable. But until then she would continue to do her job, make herself indispensable and save as much as possible for a future too murky to plan for beyond the next few weeks or months at most.

Once Deseré had gotten used to the way the office ran, they had split up the workload.

Jordan worked Mondays and Fridays with half-days the rest of the week. Deseré wasn't quite sure what he did with his time off. He seemed to spend quite a bit of it at his ranch. But whatever he did, the lines around his mouth and the dark circles under his eyes seemed to be fading a bit.

Deseré worked Tuesday through Saturday with Mondays off. On the days when Jordan wasn't working Nancy would regale Deseré with stories of his youth. Wild was a description Nancy often used.

But to Deseré's ears the stories had an edge to them, as if there was more behind Jordan's reckless behavior than a wild nature. Or maybe that's just what she wanted to hear.

She was all too aware that she had a bit of hero-worship for Jordan. What woman wouldn't when the man she lived with cooked supper? And on many nights when he could tell she'd had a particularly trying day, he did the dishes, too.

While their arrangement sounded cozy, they were fraught with underlying tension. Tension that would often awaken Deseré from her sleep. Tension that would make her yearn to feel Jordan's lips on her mouth. His hands on her thickening waist. His heart pounding beneath her ear as she laid her head on his chest. Dreams that would never come true.

Because that gentle, almost-there kiss had been a fluke. A moment out of time. And now, all these weeks later, he'd probably forgotten all about it.

Which was a good thing, right?

Not able to ignore the urge any longer, Deseré stumbled out of bed for the second time in so many hours, feeling as if her bladder was the size of an English pea.

"Well, baby James, I'll certainly be used to broken sleep when you need your night-time feedings."

After she received her first paycheck, she used her Monday off to visit an ob/gyn in Longview, who said baby James was doing just fine. The office visit and the prescription for prenatal vitamins she had refilled took a significant chunk of her paycheck, which prompted her to drop in and take a look at the hospital for low-to-no-income patients.

The facilities were clean and functional. Everyone appeared to be confident, bustling here and there with smiles on their faces. Who needed a luxurious birthing suite with decorator décor? Baby James wouldn't know the difference if he was born in a barn!

Soon. She would have to tell Jordan about James soon. But how to start that conversation?

She should have told Jordan way before now about the baby. Should have trusted that her employment status was safe. That her living arrangements were safe. That their friendship was safe.

But safe wasn't a word Deseré embraced easily. In fact, she had been getting a little paranoid lately.

She'd had two mysterious hang-up calls on her cellphone, even though Santone shouldn't have the number and a man in an expensive suit had been hanging around outside the post office last Wednesday, looking as out of place as a mardi gras ballgown at a cattle round-up. All innocent enough, except they gave her a creepy feeling down her spine each time.

And her instincts were almost always right.

Except when it came to Jordan.

There, her emotions were all over the place.

No matter how Deseré tried to stop them, both her feelings of friendship and attraction were growing. One was deep, warm and comforting. The other was frustrating beyond measure. Both were dangerously seductive.

And when the two collided...

Had it only been last week when Jordan had come in from ranch work with his back obviously hurting? As they'd sat reading, she'd offered to rub the soreness away. When her hands had slipped under his T-shirt, he'd moaned so low and deep that she hadn't been able to help moaning back.

They'd both pretended not to hear, but she'd finished that backrub right then and there and fled to her room.

By the next morning everything had been normal.

Normal, as if her palms didn't tingle from thinking about the feel of his muscles and skin under her palms.

As if she didn't bury her moans in her pillow then spend all night dreaming of him.

Frustrating. If only they didn't live together as easily as they worked together, maybe she could put some distance between them.

From kitchen duty to downtime, they were in sync with each other.

Jordan cooked; Deseré did dishes. They both liked their food hot and spicy. Neither were big on desserts. And, except for a few favorite television shows they both enjoyed, they would rather read than anything else. Hours would pass with each of them sitting in the den, engrossed in their books.

Apart from the sexual tension, it was the most comforting, relaxing, safe environment Deseré had ever lived in, and she owed it all to Jordan.

What would he think to learn she still thought about that kiss all those weeks ago?

What would he think to learn she dreamed of him at night in ways that made her ache all the way through when she woke up alone?

While washing her hands, Deseré studied her full face in the bathroom mirror. She loosened the waistband tie of her sweatpants and renewed her determination to making herself so indispensable that when Jordan found out about baby James, he would have no choice but to take her pregnancy and resulting rest days in his stride.

Because she not only needed this job, she loved this job.

As she was drying her hands, she heard it.

From Jordan's side of the bathroom door she heard him talking, although his words were indistinguishable, then heard him groaning as if he was in pain. No, that was more the sound of emotional agony than physical pain.

It was a pattern that had repeated itself too often.

She quickly slipped out of the bathroom, knowing he'd be coming in soon. Then she would hear footsteps on the stairs and, if she listened closely, she would hear the front door close behind him as he tried to outrun whatever had woken him from sleep.

Tonight she couldn't blithely go back to sleep, ignoring that the man who was fast becoming her friend was hurting.

Against the central air-conditioner's chill, she layered on her sweatshirt over the extra-large T-shirt she'd gotten free from the drug salesman last week, tugging it down across her full breasts and growing belly and trying to ignore the claustrophobic binding feeling. A little over five months.

Soon baby James would no longer be her secret and her secret alone.

She just wasn't ready yet. Wasn't ready for so much…

As she took her seat on the top step of the stair so Jordan couldn't possibly get by her without her notice, she pushed back the cringing thoughts she had about how incredibly unattractive she must look. This wasn't about abstract attraction. It was about friendship. The kind of deep friendship she'd never known before.

But how could it be? They had known each other such a short time. Surely it was too soon to call it anything more.

She had tried to cover it up by calling it lust. But unrequited lust didn't last week after week. And while lust for Jordan swirled low in her belly, love for Jordan filled her heart.

When had she begun to feel this way about Jordan? The moment she'd first seen him at the rodeo? The first time he'd cooked breakfast? The day he'd told all his patients she was an extraordinarily good nurse practitioner and they should thank their lucky stars she had agreed to serve their little backwoods community?

What was she to Jordan?

Friend? Definitely.

More?

Except for that almost-kiss she couldn't forget, he'd never indicated he felt anything for her other than…

Other than what?

And she was lying to herself. She'd caught him staring, running his eyes over her when he'd thought she wouldn't notice. But she was wise enough to know that admiration had been egged on by the extra-large bra size she now needed.

Wasn't that why he was staring?

What about the times she was sure he'd "accidentally" brushed against her? And the resulting tingle that he must have felt, too. Otherwise why would he act so startled when she "accidentally" brushed against him, too?

She knew why she did it. She craved the warmth as well as the electricity his touch built in her. Why did he reach out his hand at the same time as hers, his fingertips brushing the back of her hand or her forearm?

And then there were the times he stood close to her, as if looking over her shoulder at a chart or reaching past her for some inane object. But he would breathe in, as if he were breathing her in. And she would do the same. That melting would happen, starting around her shoulders and spreading through the rest of her body, and she would feel soft and open and vulnerable—and safe.

She'd never felt that with anyone before. Hadn't even imagined it would be possible.

So what did Jordan feel? What did he want? What did *she* want?

Knights on white horses didn't happen in real life. Jordan wasn't a knight, he was a cowboy. And his horse was a dark mahogany. Roan, he called the color. He'd named her Valkyrie.

Okay. She could live with Jordan being a Norse god instead of a white knight.

Her silliness made her grin. But her smile faded as she realized she didn't know where her fantasies stopped and reality started.

Jordan ran for all he was worth, knowing he couldn't outrun all the thoughts bombarding his mind but trying to anyway.

Yes, there was the dream that had woken him, but it had started to fade back into the shadows from which it had sprung before he could get a good hold on it to figure out what it had been about.

But he could guess.

Tomorrow—or was it today already?—was the anniversary of the day he'd killed his best friend.

Pumping his arms and legs until his heart pumped in his ears, he took a big hill with every ounce of energy he could pour into it. Running wouldn't help with these thoughts and vague, faulty memories, but it would help with the restlessness, the vibrations inside him that threatened to shake him apart.

How could no one else see the frantic unrhythmic explosion of nerve endings, the random popping of synapses inside him as one memory piled onto another and another until finally every soldier he'd ever failed to return home hale and whole stared at him, mocking his failure.

Think about the successes. Think about something else. Think about something that makes you feel good about yourself. That's what his therapist was telling him.

Deseré. He thought about Deseré, thought about the admiring way she looked at him when he'd charmed a child out of being afraid of his tongue depressor, about the way she smelled with her hair still damp, about the warmth that built in him whenever she stood near him. About the fire she started in him whenever she touched him.

Now he could draw in a deep breath, loosen his shoulders, lengthen his stride and bear to turn around and head back home, back to the bed he dreaded crawling into.

How would he feel if he knew Deseré awaited him in his bed?

But she'd already had experience with a man who couldn't make a stable home for her. Her growing belly was proof of that.

He couldn't even begin to ask her to take him on with all the problems he was working out.

But he *was* working them out.

His concentration was better. He could feel again without being overwhelmed with a heaviness that had made feeling anything impossible only a few months before. He could even laugh on occasion.

Deseré, with her quiet acceptance, her easy calmness and her exquisite sexiness, which had first brought him out of his apathy, was the reason why he now had hope that someday he would be okay in his own skin again.

Maybe someday he could even be okay enough for her.

He headed toward his own driveway with hope giving extra energy to each step.

Bang!

The noise had his heart racing as he hit the ditch, feeling the coldness of the night seep through his shorts and T-shirt as a nervous sweat covered him. He reached for a sidearm that wasn't there, ready to defend himself against—

Against a metal trash-can lid that had blown loose into the side of a car.

As he fought to get his breathing under control, to slow his heart rate, to make his mind work in an orderly fashion, instead of sending disjointed clips of memory racing behind his eyes.

He wasn't okay. He was far from it.

He wasn't fit to be Deseré's anything.

On trembling legs he walked the last few yards to his front door, ignoring the nausea and the tunnel vision that had come with his abrupt adrenaline surge.

A shower and a book would take care of the rest of the night.

And he would have to let tomorrow take care of itself. There was only so much he could handle at a time.

Deseré must have dozed. As she heard the opening of the front door she found herself leaning against the wall. Her neck and shoulders ached because her head had fallen against that same wall at an awkward angle.

Hoping her smile was more welcome than a grimace, she waited for Jordan to look up and notice her.

His face was grim, his movements ungraceful.

He must have sensed her because he jerked his attention in her direction with alarm. That alarm quickly turned into a glare. But she'd seen a glimpse of sadness, loss and despair before the flatness had come down to hide it.

"I woke you." His voice was as flat as his eyes.

She brushed it off. "No biggie."

"You need your rest."

"And you don't?" She softened her response. "Tomorrow's Sunday. We can both sleep in."

She swallowed, realizing he could have interpreted what she'd said as if she was implying they would be sleeping together. He stood still in the shadows, giving no indication what he thought.

She didn't know how to fix it without making it worse.

Then he moved into the light she'd turned on. His shorts and T-shirt were stained with grass and mud. His shin had a scrape than ran the long length of it. And he was shivering.

Catching the stair rail, she pulled herself up. "You're hurt?"

"No."

Before she could stop herself, she winced at his sharpness.

And he grimaced at her reaction.

"Why are you here, Deseré?"

Did he mean on his staircase or in Piney Woods? Or was it a great existential question, like why was she there in his life?

She chose the easy answer. "I heard you get up and leave."

"And you chose to sit here in the cold in the middle of the night and wait for me to get back home." He narrowed his eyes at her. "Why?"

"Because I…" She hesitated, searching for a word big enough, all-encompassing enough, but couldn't find the right one. "I care."

"Well, don't."

"Don't care?"

He nodded his confirmation. "Don't care."

All her emotional conflict resolved itself in anger. "You don't get to tell me who I can and can't care for. I'll choose my own friends, thank you very much. And you're it." She realized she was yelling so she said more softly, "You're my friend."

To make her point, she crossed her arms, very aware they no longer folded easily across her expanding chest. "And there's nothing you can do to change that."

He gave her a twisted grin. The flatness in his eyes changed to unmistakable sadness. "I wish that were true."

He took three steps up, then stopped and looked at her, where she was determined not to move out of his way. "Good night, Deseré."

Still she stood there. He would have to pass by her, have to brush against her, have to touch her to get to his room.

And she needed that touch, needed it to know he was okay. Needed it to know she was okay.

When he continued to stand there, waiting for her to move away, she took three steps down, meeting him halfway.

The difference in steps put their chins on an equal level.

She had intended to reach out and put her hand on his shoulder in a gesture of comfort. Instead, she found herself leaning forward. She placed her lips on his.

Although his mouth had looked hard, his lips were warm and soft.

And they moved against hers as his arm came up around her, pulling her into him.

Before she could stop herself, she moaned as she swayed into him. His arms steadied her.

She pushed her tongue between his lips and he let her. Then he lifted his head, turning away enough so that their lips were no longer lined up. With a gentle hand he turned her round, putting his hand in the small of her back to get her moving up the stairs.

She followed his direction, although vaguely she realized if she hadn't been so dazed by that kiss, she would have protested.

He walked her to her door, with his hand guiding her and warming her, and even opened her bedroom door for her.

If she reached back and caught his hand, would he

follow her in to her room? Into her bed? Was that really what she wanted?

Ever so gently, his big, solid hand put pressure on her back, encouraging her to step forward.

As soon as she crossed the threshold, he dropped his hand and she felt chilled and alone.

But then he leaned in close to her ear and breathed deeply.

His voice husky and deep, he whispered, "Good night, friend."

And closed the door between them.

CHAPTER EIGHT

CLOSING THAT DOOR between them had been both the easiest and the hardest thing he'd ever done.

Jordan sat on the edge of his bed, knowing sleep would be nearly impossible.

Instead, he made his way downstairs, to the unfinished room that should have been hers.

He studied the new rolls of wallpaper. A nondescript beige with no personality. So wrong in every way.

Friends. The word bounced through Jordan's head as he began to strip the last of the old paper from the walls.

Once that task was completed, it was well past midnight and he willed himself to stop. Maybe he could get in a few hours of rest. He stretched and yawned, making his way upstairs and climbing underneath sheets and a blanket that no longer felt so ominously threatening.

They smelled of the fabric softener Deseré had started buying. They smelled of comfort and refuge.

Friends. The last word on his mind when he went to sleep and the first one on his mind when he woke up.

But in the stark light of morning the word cut as well as comforted.

Why couldn't he be satisfied with just being friends? Why did he have to want, crave, more?

That craving made him edgy as he listened for

sounds from the shared bathroom, heard none and took a quick cold shower.

Hopefully, Deseré *would* sleep in. She'd been up too late for her stage of pregnancy.

Jordan broke and whisked enough eggs for breakfast for the two of them. He would scramble them on the stove when Deseré came downstairs. Deseré would make the toast, like she always did.

She was the perfect roommate. Not only did they both enjoy the same televisions shows but they both liked their quiet time to read, too. Before he'd met Deseré, he'd thought it was a calm he could only find by himself.

But with Deseré the silence between them was comfortable, pleasant and anything but lonely. Sitting in the den together, with the flipping of pages being the only sounds, fed his soul in a way he hadn't known was possible.

He never wanted it to end. Jordan pulled himself up short at that thought.

If he had told her about Brad, if he told her what he'd done, would he lose her?

He squeezed his eyes shut and ground his jaw. *He didn't know what he would do without her.*

And that thought made panic rise up in him. He took a deep breath, deliberately turning his thoughts away from the reasons for his near panic attack. He took deep breaths, concentrating on the here and now, on the eggs he stirred, on the birds outside, on the sounds of Deseré coming down the stairs.

He wanted better for Deseré than he could give her. But, then, she didn't want him except as a friend, did she?

He was damned fortunate she wanted a friendship between them. So why couldn't it be enough?

It wasn't like he had an overabundance of friends.

Rusty and Plato were about the extent of them. One of them was related to him and they were both employed by him, so should that even count?

Then again, Deseré was employed by him, too. But he was certain that had no bearing on their friendship, just as with Rusty and Plato.

Jordan had never been friends with a woman before.

But Deseré and he talked. They talked about their patients and about the little things that went on in town and about the televisions shows they watched together and about the ranch he had yet to take her to and anything else that came up—except her past and his military experiences.

By unspoken mutual agreement, they both steered clear of those topics.

And then there was the baby growing in her belly. She was obviously showing. And the morning sickness that had been fairly hard to ignore hadn't abated until a few weeks ago.

Jordan struggled with whether to mention the elephant in the room or allowing Deseré her privacy.

At the sound of her footsteps he turned round from scooping up the eggs. Her eyes looked tired today. He should take more of her shifts and start giving her more days off.

"Morning," he said.

"I'm pregnant." Her voice broke.

He ignored the break.

"I know." He put her plate on the table, too aware that his conflicting thoughts had come through in his short response. But there was no such things as a do-over, was there?

She stopped, frozen. Her mouth worked but nothing came out.

He poured two glasses of milk and set them on the table. "Could you put grape jelly on my toast this morning instead of that orange marmalade stuff you like?"

"You know?"

"I'm trained to notice that kind of thing, remember?" He glanced at the toaster as an excuse to look away. Highly charged emotions weren't his thing.

"How long?"

"I would guess five months."

"Yes, five and a little more." Her hand touched her belly. "No, I mean how long have you known?"

He shrugged. "A while, I guess."

"Why didn't you say anything?"

Now he turned round, leaving behind all pretense of keeping this conversation casual.

"Say what, Deseré? Trust me? Like that would work. Have you ever trusted someone because they told you to? Or maybe I should have said something like, 'I can help you through this.' But, then, that goes back to that trust thing, doesn't it?"

His voice was getting stronger, firmer, maybe even agitated. But something deep inside him had decided to come out and he couldn't seem to stop it. "I thought we had something here, some kind of a connection. But, no, every day is the same. We co-exist. That's it. Just two bodies sharing the same space."

Bodies. Hers set him on fire. To rein himself in he mentioned the baby. "Make that three bodies, one of which you failed to mention because..." He scrubbed his hand through his hair. "Why, Deseré? What did you think I'd do? What did you think I'd say? Did you think I would judge you? Me? Who has lived through the censure of everyone I know?"

Looking at the raw anguish in Jordan's face almost broke her heart. But self-preservation won through.

"Trust, Jordan? What do you know of trust?" She propped her hands on her hips. "Do you know how many nights I've heard you cry out in your sleep? Do you know how many times I've stood on the opposite side of your locked door, wanting to go to you, to comfort you, to chase away your nightmares? But have you trusted me with anything that really means anything to you?"

Baby James chose that moment to kick her hard in the kidneys. Apparently, he didn't approve of her raised voice, of her agitated state. She took a deep breath, trying to calm herself.

She reached for courage to ask, "So where does that leave us?" and found her world stop as she waited for his answer.

He looked away from her, his shoulders sagging, then turned back and looked her square in the eyes with his chin held high.

"Friends." He nodded and said it again. "We're friends."

He turned back to put butter into the skillet on the stove. "I haven't had a lot of practice, though, so I may screw up from time to time."

The muscles in his neck stood out, exposing the strain he was trying to hide.

She opened the refrigerator to hunt for the marmalade and jelly. From inside the cold depths, she answered him. "Neither have I, on the practice thing. But I'd like to get better at it."

When she turned round with the jars in her hands,

he was holding the skillet away from the flames and looking at her.

"Me, too," he said. And his smile was both hopeful and pleading at the same time.

"I'll pick up milk today. Anything else we need?" He threw away the empty milk container and picked up a mug of hot tea.

"Bananas, please. I've been craving them lately."

"Are you having leg cramps? Is your potassium level okay? You're taking your prenatal vitamins, right?"

"No leg cramps. Yes, I'm taking my vitamins. Can't a pregnant lady simply like bananas?"

"You're seeing an ob/gyn regularly, right?"

"Yes, I've been driving to Dallas on my days off."

"The baby is okay?"

"He's perfect."

"Let me know when your next appointment is and I'll drive over with you."

She grinned, warmed all the way through at the protectiveness in his voice. "I'm fine to drive myself."

"But I want to." He raised his eyebrow. "I care for you."

"Okay." She put her hand on his shoulder as she passed behind him. Impulsively, she rose up on tiptoe and planted a kiss at the base of his neck. "Thanks."

Under her palm, Jordan stilled, not even breathing. Deseré held her own breath until Jordan drew in a lungful of air.

"You're welcome. It's what friends do."

"Could I have the butter, please?" Deseré held out her hand, mindful of the way Jordan brushed his fingers along hers as he handed her the butter tray.

Would she ever get used to that tingle when they touched? Did Jordan feel it, too? Friends. More?

She made a decision and took a risk.

"Last night was rough." Deseré spread butter and jelly on his toast and then her own, trying to keep strong emotion from her voice. Nothing made Jordan back off quicker than high emotion.

Deseré knew what came next. Something impersonal. Something distracting. Something that made Jordan feel safely in control.

But Jordan wasn't in control, was he? His nightmares were.

"You shouldn't get up. I'll try to be quieter." He washed out the skillet and put it away. "The downstairs room will be done soon. I won't disturb you when you move down there."

"No hurry. I'm content where I am." More than content. Being so close to Jordan, she felt comfortable and safe.

She took a swallow of tea to wet her throat, determined to see this conversation through.

"The dreams. Nightmares from your time in the army, right?" She continued before he could deny it. She didn't want to put him in a position to lie to her. She was already walking a thin line as it was. "Do you think you might have PTSD? You can get help."

With a fork full of eggs poised halfway to his mouth, he stopped and looked at her, shaking his head.

She could see it in his eyes. He was on the verge of talking. If she was just patient enough...

Very deliberately, he took a bite, chewed and swallowed while she waited, trying not to turn her watchfulness into an awkward stare.

He drew his fork through his leftover eggs. "I got the paper stripped off the walls last night. I'm thinking we might want to go with different paper and paint. That beige seems too dull."

Exasperated at his deliberate shift in conversation, she plopped her toast onto her plate and crossed her arms. "You want to talk about wallpaper?"

He nodded, taking a sip of his tea and totally ignoring the frustration she was broadcasting as clearly as she could.

"I was thinking you might want to pick it out. We'll need to order it from the feed store. It may take a week or so for it to come in."

"You have nightmares that drive you from your bed—from your house—and you want to talk about wallpaper?"

She broke off to catch her breath while he sat, swirling his mug of cooling tea in his hands, studying the motion as it made circular waves almost as if he was hypnotizing himself, taking himself away from here, away from *her*.

"Fine. Don't talk."

As she began noisily stacking her silverware on her plate, he reached over, putting his hand over her wrist. "Deseré…"

He looked away, up to the ceiling over her head. "I thought, if you're really okay keeping the room you're in, we might fix up the downstairs room for the baby."

All her emotion gathered into a large ball and dropped into her stomach.

As her eyes filled with tears, he looked down from the ceiling and into her face.

"I've been seeing a therapist on my days off. For the baby. He's going to need a stable home life. I'm going to do everything I can to give that to him."

Deseré wanted to say—she wasn't really sure what

she wanted to say. But it didn't matter since she couldn't swallow past the lump in her throat to respond.

He twirled his cup again, sloshing tea over the rim. "It's not PTSD, at least not yet. My therapist has labeled it acute stress response for now. It doesn't become full-blown chronic PTSD unless it goes on for more than ninety days. We're close to that place on the timeline, but as I've been showing improvement we're holding off on calling it anything more."

He took a sip and she echoed his movements. Her dry throat appreciated the liquid, although her stomach was still thinking about it.

He held her gaze the whole time and she didn't dare look away. Not when his eyes were pleading for her to stay connected.

The half-smile she gave him as encouragement seemed to do the trick as he returned it and put his mug back on the table.

Jordan felt the floor stop shifting beneath him, allowing him to find a precarious balance.

He could do this. Deseré *was* his friend and he trusted her. Trusted her enough to not think less of him because of his weaknesses. Trusted her enough to not use his weakness against him. Almost trusted her enough to tell her more.

"It's not all about my time away." Time away. It was what he felt most comfortable calling those three tours of duty. "It's about…" He swallowed another sip of tea, feeling the too-tight muscles in his throat work against each other. He had to look down at his plate to get this next part out. "Some other stuff that happened when I was a teenager." Without raising his head, he watched from under his lashes, ready to look away before she could pierce him with a spear-like look.

But this was Deseré. She wouldn't do that—would she?

"You've probably already heard about it. Too many people still talk about it."

"No, I haven't." She dragged her fork through the eggs on her plate without looking at them. Instead, she kept her gaze fixed on him. "I've heard about how wild you were. And there's an undertone I don't understand, but I didn't know anything in particular that happened."

She'd left the conversation wide-open for him to explain. He could tell her. Get it out between them. Test their bonds of friendship. And risk losing the best thing that had ever happened to him.

"There's a storm front coming in tonight. Drastic temperature drops. Sleet. Hail. Possible tornadoes. I'm going out to the ranch to secure everything I can tie down."

"Weather? We're going to talk about the weather now?"

"It's all I can handle right now, okay?"

Silently, she stared at him as if she was trying to see inside his soul. She licked her lips and he was so hot for her he had to shift in his chair to keep himself from coming out of it.

He'd never been into pregnant women before, but he was into her. What would she be like in his bed? *There you go, Hart. Divert this heavy emotional scene by thinking about sex.*

"Okay," she said.

Okay? Had he said something about sex out loud?

It took his head a few seconds to catch up as he realized she'd agreed to back off her emotional probing. For now.

She was the kind of woman who wouldn't let something go. Stubborn. He liked that about her. She would never give up on anything she cared about.

She'd told him she cared about him.

Did that mean that *anything* included him?

He hoped so.

"Do you want to drive out with me?" he surprised himself by asking. Of course she didn't. His ex had made it all too clear that hay and horse manure were not the way to woo a woman.

"Sure."

"Okay." He realized he was grinning as if she *had* just agreed to have sex with him.

Have sex. With Deseré it would be making love.

"You'll need your coat," he cautioned her.

"I don't think so. It's barely chilly outside. Besides—" she grinned "—I've got my belly to keep me warm. Pregnancy seems to have turned me warm-natured."

If they had been more than friends, he would have made an insinuating quip about how hot her body was to him. Instead, he said, "It will be cold by the time we get home tonight. The temperature is likely to drop twenty or so degrees by then."

She frowned, skeptical. "In east Texas? How does that work?"

"Warm air from the Gulf Stream meets cold air from the Arctic front. We're in an area that gets it a couple times each fall and sometimes in the spring, too" He picked up both their plates. "As soon as I get the dishes done, we'll leave. You might want to add a hat and gloves to that coat."

As she bit her lip, he realized the problem. "It's okay, Deseré, I've got to stop by the feed store on the way out of town. We'll pick up a coat for you there."

Deseré thought of the small amount of money she'd been stockpiling for medical bills for herself and the baby. "Maybe I should just stay here."

"I want you to come." Jordan turned off the water and dried his hands on the kitchen towel. "Please."

Her pride said no, she couldn't afford to. But deep inside she knew Jordan wasn't a man who said please easily or often. And she couldn't say no to him. Not now. Not ever.

Friends. Maybe it was enough for him. But it was way too little for her.

But that was her problem, wasn't it? Not his problem at all.

She touched her belly. He'd offered to help—sort of.

Her heart sank as she reminded herself it was her problem. Not his at all.

CHAPTER NINE

THE FEED STORE was a place of wonder. It was every discount store Deseré had ever seen all scrunched into one small space.

She thought about checking out the wallpaper sample books, but then decided she'd rather look at them with Jordan by her side. That he wanted to make a home for her son was a concept that kept growing and growing inside her like a bubble of pure joy.

As Jordan drove his truck round past the public entrance to supervise the loading of supplies "out back", Deseré wandered among the scented candles and saddles and jewelry and baby clothes and a display of bananas. From a rack of women's coats she pulled off a soft pink one and tried it on. Swing-coat style, it fit perfectly for her expanding middle. After checking the price tag, she put it back. Instead, she drifted over to a counter with a sale sign, chose a man's thick, thermal-lined hoodie and tucked it under her arm.

Then, to waste time, she wandered toward the women's clothing section with its single rack of maternity clothes squeezed between the junior-size skinny jeans and the more matronly boot-cut ones.

At this time last year, if someone had suggested that Deseré would be lusting after a pair of pants with a stretchy tummy panel, she would have called them crazy.

But even without tying her scrubs, the band dug into her waist. And it would only get worse before it got better.

With a mixture of reluctance and relief she added a functional pair of pregnancy jeans to the hoodie and set them both on the cash register counter.

The sales clerk gave her an acknowledging nod. "Will that be all?"

"Yes, but first would you point me to the restroom, please?"

"Yes, ma'am. Straight back past the lava lamps and sleeping bags then turn right. The door says 'Employees Only', but just ignore that."

Lava lamps? Deseré didn't have much time to ponder them as she picked up her pace toward the restroom.

When she came out again, Jordan was waiting for her as he checked out the sleeping bags.

"Waiting for me long?"

"Not long," he lied. He'd gotten worried when he hadn't been able to find her in the store. Ever since the pregnancy had come out in the open between them, he'd felt his protective urges go into overtime. "Are you okay?"

"Fine." She pointed to the lava lamp next to the sleeping bag he'd been inspecting. "I like the green one with all the glitter floating in it."

"And here I thought you'd go for the yellow one with the globs of blue swirling around." He gave her a grin. Deseré made him do that—grin—more than anyone he'd ever known before.

She walked past him, brushing against him in the

tight space then almost knocking her favorite lamp off the shelf as she jerked away.

Jordan wasn't sure what to think of that reaction. Should he be flattered or insulted? Either way, he knew she wasn't neutral about him.

"Easy." Deliberately, he caught hold of her arm to steady her.

This time she didn't try to move away. In fact, for the slightest of seconds he could have sworn she leaned into him instead.

"I'm okay." Then she let him hold onto her as she led him toward the counter. "I need to pay."

"Already done." They were close enough to the cash-register counter for him to grab the large sack without breaking stride. "Don't make an issue of it, okay?"

Swallowing down her protests, she came up with a wavering smile. "Okay. Thank you."

He gave her an acknowledging nod. "Ready to get going?"

She eyed the sack. "Did a bit of shopping yourself?"

"Yup. I do most of my shopping here. If Monroe's Feed and Seed ain't got it, I don't need it." He looked closely at her as he said it. The first time he'd said that to his ex she had given him a sick little laugh then turned pale as she'd realized he'd meant it.

But Deseré gave him one of those smiles that lit his world as she said, "Ain't that the truth?", matching both his vernacular and his sincerity.

"Not much of a shopper?" he pushed as he opened the truck door for her.

She took his extended hand as she climbed up into the truck. "Never have been."

As they often did, they fell into a safe, comfortable

silence. Too rarely in his life had Jordan found a friend who knew that words weren't always necessary.

Brad had been one of those friends. Up until the day Jordan had killed him.

Pain squeezed Jordan's heart. Almost twenty years ago, yet some days it still hurt like it had been yesterday.

As if she knew he was in agony, she reached her hand across the truck and laid it, palm up, on the console that separated them.

Lightly, loosely, Jordan rested his hand on hers, palm to palm.

He stole a glance at her, but she was looking out the passenger-side window, giving him what he needed without taking from him what he couldn't give.

Jordan had never been so grateful for the quiet acceptance.

As they listened to the radio, the warmth of her hand in his warmed his heart, making the agonizing clenching ease.

And today, of all days, didn't seem so bad after all.

Grateful for the warmth of the hoodie, Deseré sat on a stump as Rusty leaned against a fence, flexing his fingers from the sling that held his arm still.

"I hate this helpless feeling," he said.

Deseré watched as one of the mares jerked her head, pulling taut the rope Jordan had just thrown over her neck.

The calm, quiet rumble of Jordan's voice carried to her on a cold gust. Although the sun shone brightly in the clear sky, the wind was picking up and the temperature was falling.

She gave Rusty a sympathetic smile. "Compound fractures take a while to heal completely."

"I'll finish up that guest room as soon as I can."

"No hurry. Jordan's working on it, little by little." The thought of Jordan making the room into a nursery filled her with a sense of wholeness and security she would never had imagined before now.

Rusty gave her a long look as if he could see inside her.

Clearing his throat, he said, "I hope you don't mind me saying so, but you've been really good for Jordan."

A burst of joy exploded in her, warming her more than an on-sale hoodie ever could. But she really didn't know what to say to that in reply.

Before she could think of a response Rusty continued, "For this to be such a hard day for Jordan, he's getting through it really well. I think we've all got you to thank for that."

In the pasture Plato shooed away a bigger horse so Jordan could rope the next mare.

"They're kind of wild, with the storm coming in. It doesn't help with that big buck stallion being so protective." Rusty looked out, watching Plato and Jordan do the work he usually did. "That stallion isn't usually much for letting anyone or anything near him. I keep telling Jordan he's more trouble than he's worth, but he's a good breeder and once the mares are pregnant, his whole attitude changes. He barely lets those mares out of his sight."

As if he could feel himself being watched, Jordan looked over, giving her a smile and a nod.

Rusty grinned at her. "Kind of like another stud I know."

A hundred thoughts popped into Deseré's mind, but the one that popped out was, "So what is everyone saying about me being pregnant?"

Rusty gave her a surprised look that failed miserably. "You're pregnant?"

She smirked back at him. "No. I'm only fat in my midsection."

"My momma taught me to never assume a woman's pregnant just because she looks it."

"Wise momma."

He nodded. "Yes, ma'am. She is." He flexed his fingers again. "She'd like you to come for Thanksgiving dinner. It will be the first one in three years that Jordan's been home for."

"He told me he was in Afghanistan for three tours of duty. He's missed a lot of holidays, hasn't he?"

"Yes, he has."

"Is that why today is so bad for him? Something happened over there?"

Rusty's eyes turned bleak. "No."

Then he turned his attention back to the men working the horses in the pasture.

She thought that was all he would say. But then he squared his shoulders and turned back to her. "I'm not sure I should be telling you this."

"Then maybe you shouldn't."

"I feel worse not telling you. I think you'll understand and, heaven knows, he needs someone who understands him." Rusty rubbed his eyes. "When Jordan was eighteen there was an accident. It was a stupid, teenage thing but, well, his best friend, Brad, died. Today is the anniversary of that death."

Sympathy for Jordan's pain made her throat thicken. "That must have been devastating."

"Yeah. It still is." He flexed his fingers. "Jordan trusts you. He needs to talk about it. Maybe you could ask him."

"I don't know if he really trusts me that well."

"He brought you here."

"So?"

Rusty must have read the confusion on her face. "He's never brought anyone here before. Not even his ex when they were at their hottest and heaviest. This ranch is his safe place. Only Plato and I come out here. And his sister when she has vet duties. Otherwise even she steers clear, respecting Jordan's boundaries."

"Safe places and boundaries?" Hearing a cowhand like Rusty spout pop-psychology reminded Deseré to keep away from stereotypes and labeling.

He grinned at her. "My girlfriend's a high-school counselor. She uses words like safe place and boundaries so often I've pretty much picked up the lingo."

Deseré watched Jordan slowly lay the gentlest of hands on a mare's nose, steadying her with his own steadiness.

Feeling like she was indulging in gossip, the kind she didn't want people indulging in where she was concerned, she asked anyway, "So what was Jordan like, growing up? I keep hearing he was wild, but nobody will say exactly what that means."

Rusty stared out at Jordan, too. He stared so long his silence started to feel like he was condemning her for asking.

Almost, she shrugged off the question. But she was learning that these cowboy types required as much patience as the animals they tended and if she bided her time, Rusty would eventually talk.

She counted her breaths, getting to forty-three before Rusty spoke.

"It was like he was two different kids. One was the kid who was always defying authority. Take football,

for instance. He'd do things like make his own calls on
the football field instead of the ones the coach told him
to play. Stay out past midnight when coach set curfew
for ten. It was like he dared anyone to kick him off the
team. Of course, nobody would. He was Dean Hart's
son. And Dean Hart was the most generous Booster
Club contributor this town's ever had."

"Do you think he might not have wanted to play?"

Rusty scratched his head. "He really didn't have
much of a choice. His dad wanted him to play, so that
was it."

"And rodeo? Nancy told me he injured himself bull-
riding."

"He was good with riding the junior rodeo circuit."
Rusty paused, as if he was deciding to say more.

Deseré waited while she watched Jordan manipu-
late the controls of his tractor to drop a bale of hay into
the back of an old beat-up farm truck and give Plato
a thumbs-up to move out to a farther pasture with it.

Finally, Rusty finished his thought. "I think he was
into rodeo because it took him away from his parents.
He got to be on the road most of his summers that way."

"By himself?"

"Not always." Rusty grinned. "We grow up fast
out here in Texas. It's not unusual for us to get our
driver's license the day we turn sixteen—fifteen, if we
get a farm license—then head out the next day pulling
a six-place horse trailer. We've all been driving since
we could touch the pedals and see over the steering-
wheel while sitting on a phone book. Besides, rodeo
folks take care of each other. If he'd needed something,
somebody would have been there for him." Rusty added
as an afterthought, "More so on the road than at home.

I guess you think that's pretty young to be so independent, huh?"

"My sister and I were practically on our own ever since our mother died."

"How old were you then?"

"I was ten and Celeste was twelve. But we weren't totally on our own until Hurricane Katrina took our dad. Celeste was eighteen by then and kept me from being placed in a foster home or becoming a ward of the state. So I understand growing up fast. I can see that kind of independence and maturity in Jordan. But that doesn't fit with the wild-child stories I keep hearing. Not just the rebellion against authority but the drinking and reckless driving everyone whispers about."

Rusty shrugged his shoulder then stood restlessly. "That's one you need to ask Jordan about." He looked down at her, his eyes going soft and hopeful. "He needs to talk about so much. Maybe you'll be the one."

He reached down his good hand for her. "Looks like they're finishing up here."

She took the offered hand, very aware of the extra weight she was carrying. But the easy way he pulled her up showed her baby weight was no problem for him.

Valkyrie, the horse Deseré remembered from the rodeo, seemed reluctant to be led into the barn. Jordan looped his arm over her neck and whispered in her large triangular ear, making it twitch. Putting his hand on her near withers, he coaxed her to move with him.

"Jordan's always loved animals."

Deseré nodded. That she knew. "So why didn't Jordan become a veterinarian, like his sister?"

"That's another one of those deep-seated Jordan issues. To tell the truth, I'd just be guessing anyway. Add that to your list of things to talk about."

"I can't imagine Jordan voluntarily talking about anything of importance to him."

"Would you try? Please?" Rusty must have heard more in her voice than she'd meant to show because he put his arm around her shoulder and pulled her in for a hug. "And if he won't open up at first, hang in there. He's worth the effort."

"Hey!" Jordan called as he latched the barn door closed. "Everything okay over there?"

When Deseré would have pulled away, Rusty pulled her in tighter instead. "Just keeping Miss Deseré warm."

Jordan narrowed his eyes at both of them. "I left the keys in the truck if you want to turn the heater on," he directed at her.

"I'm fine," she called back, squirming free of Rusty's hold.

"We'll be through here in a few minutes."

"Really, I'm fine."

"Sooner if Rusty would quit flapping his jaws and help out a little." Jordan pointed to a bucket hanging on a nail outside the barn. "The brood mares could use a cup or two of oats, if you can free up your unbroken arm long enough to scoop from the oats bin."

"On it, boss." With a wink Rusty loped toward the bucket before disappearing into the part of the barn sectioned off to hold the various types of feed they portioned out to the horses.

Without Rusty to distract her, Deseré realized how cold those strong gusts were getting.

She climbed into the truck, started it up and turned the heater on. The rumbling underscored the song on the radio, some plaintive cowgirl singing about the man that got away.

That's what men do, honey. That's what Celeste

would have told her. Celeste had certainly had enough experience with men to see that pattern time and time again, including in her marriage where she had suspected that Santone had been unfaithful time and time again for the ego-thrilling power of it.

That's what Deseré believed, too.

But somehow she couldn't make that love-'em-and-leave-'em image fit where Jordan was concerned.

Friends. With benefits?

Deseré rubbed her belly. Not for her.

Her baby deserved stability. And so did she.

Finally, another song started up, this one about going fishing. She liked it much better.

Jordan was in the barn. He'd bought the sleeping bag he'd been inspecting at the feed store earlier and was storing it in the tack room, along with an air mattress and pump.

The thought that he would be spending more time sleeping at the ranch made her feel incredibly sad and relieved at the same time. If the tension at the house didn't let up soon…

She had no idea what would happen.

And their conversation that morning was sure to have some backlash, especially if she followed through on what Rusty wanted and tried to talk to Jordan.

Jordan would try to put distance between them, or maybe she would be the one to back away. It was probably the best way to handle the attraction they kept trying to ignore.

But it was a temporary solution.

If only she could think of a more permanent one, she would go for it.

Images of Jordan and her cuddled together flooded her mind and Deseré pushed them away.

Fantasies had their place, but not when she was trying to figure out what to do in real life.

Her cellphone buzzed, showing a number she didn't recognize. No message—again.

Since she had the cheapest plan with just enough minutes for emergencies, she didn't bother to call back. The last two had resulted in nothing but a voice mail with the name of some firm she'd never heard of.

She tried to push down her paranoia with logic. Why would Santone go to the bother of finding her? He'd only wanted her to step into her sister's place to save face in front of all his friends, right? He'd wanted to show how magnanimous he was to his dead wife's sister.

Her instincts told her she was wrong. He'd wanted more than that. He'd said she owed him for all the money he'd spent on the in vitro pregnancy. He'd even hinted that he owned both her and her son.

A twinge of fear made her shake.

"Still cold?" Jordan slid inside, closed the truck door, and turned the thermostat higher. He caught her hands in his, rubbing them, then turned and pulled the sack from behind the seat. Inside, she saw the pink swing coat she'd admired, along with the maternity jeans, several shirts and a dress she'd been looking at. He pulled gloves from the bottom of the sack.

"You bought all those?" On the heels of Santone wanting to own her, her tone wasn't as gracious as it could have been.

Jordan scowled as he shoved the sack back over the seat. "Part of your room and board."

"Since when has clothing ever come under that heading?"

"Since I obviously don't pay you enough to buy what

you need." He put the truck in gear and headed for the highway.

"You pay me what we agreed on. I'm saving up for medical expenses for the baby." She put the gloves on. The fleece warmed her fingers, but not as much as Jordan's hands had. "You should take the cost of these out of my next paycheck. I'll take the rest of it back."

His jaw jutted out. "No, you won't."

"I won't?" This argument was just what she needed to keep her mind off the worries she had no solution for. "You're my boss, not my keeper."

That muscle worked in Jordan's jaw, even though he kept his eyes on the road. Finally, he swallowed. She could see by the bobbing of his throat that whatever he'd swallowed down must have been a mouthful.

"The clothes are gifts, okay?" He glanced over at her before turning his attention back to the road. His tone was soft and seductive. "Just say okay."

When he asked so sweetly, how could she say anything else? "Okay."

CHAPTER TEN

AFTER A QUICK trip to fill the truck's dual tanks with gas, they headed home to beat the darkening skies and howling wind.

Deseré kept glancing at him, obviously nervous.

"It's okay. Just a storm." He clamped down tight to keep from adding, *I'll keep you safe.*

That would imply too much.

Too much for him or for her?

He cranked up the radio so he wouldn't have to think about it. His therapist would not have been pleased at his choice of coping skill.

Deseré cooked while Jordan took care of the outside work. Grilled cheese sandwiches and canned tomato soup. Compared to Jordan's cooking, hers felt inadequate. *She* felt inadequate.

She wanted to do more. Help in some way. And not just tonight in the house. But every night in Jordan's head.

Which rhymed too neatly with *in Jordan's bed*.

And neither place was where she should be.

Jordan didn't need her, no matter what Rusty had said. The way he'd avoided having a conversation with her as they drove home proved that.

She touched her growing belly.

Soon, very soon, she would have her hands full of someone who needed her. Someone to take care of.

But who would take care of her? As quickly as the question forced itself on her, the answer came. *Jordan would do it.*

In the midst of giving herself a strong sermon on standing on her own two feet, she jumped as the door burst open with a blast of wild, freezing wind along with the scent of warm male. It totally derailed her private discussion on independence.

"Supper smells great." Jordan rubbed his hands together, lathering up under the kitchen faucet.

"Hot tea?"

"That would be perfect."

For a moment, only the slightest of seconds, Deseré had the strongest desire to take two steps forward, go up on her toes, lean in two inches and kiss him as if he were her man, come in from the cold.

She turned to the stove to pour boiling water from a kettle over a tea bag resting in a coffee mug.

It was a good thing she had a reason to turn away before he could see her face. She had no idea what expression she was broadcasting, but it couldn't be the calm, confident, self-contained one she wanted to show him. She wasn't that good an actress.

As Jordan took the plate of sandwiches and the oversize mugs of soup to the table, the lights flickered, dimmed, but then came back strongly.

"I couldn't get the generator to crank. So, just in case…" He pulled out an old-fashioned oil lamp from the hall closet, lit it and set it in the middle of the table.

At the exact moment he set down the lamp the lights

flickered one last time and then the house was plunged into darkness.

The effect was quaint and rustic and too charming for Deseré to ignore the romanticism of it all. Although she counted on the soft lamplight to cover any emotion that might spill out into her body language.

What would it be like to be herself, completely, without restrictions? Why did Jordan make her want to be that vulnerable?

As they sat across from each other, the table they ate at together every morning and every night seemed to have shrunk in size to only the circle of light, a light that dimmed and danced, flickered and shadowed the farther it tried to reach outside the circle.

Jordan's face was cast as all angles and planes and deep-set eyes by the simple lamplight.

She probably looked round and starkly pale.

But it didn't really matter, did it?

She sipped at her soup. "Maybe they'll come back on in a few minutes, huh?"

Jordan shrugged. "Doesn't matter, does it? We're set for the night." He chewed a bite of his sandwich. "This is good."

"It's just grilled cheese." She brushed away the compliment. "How long before the house gets cold? Socks and sweats for bed tonight, I guess." And didn't that present a lovely image?

His sipped at his soup, looking up over the rim of the oversize cup to meet her eyes. His brown eyes seemed to sparkle and dim by turns as the lamplight wavered. "I'll light the wood in the fireplace after we eat. If we stay downstairs in the den, that should keep us warm."

With her mouth full she nodded while the image of

the two of them sharing an intimate fire took full bloom in her imagination. The sandwich was hard to swallow.

Something about the setting made them both linger over their supper, taking breaths between bites, opening their eyes wide to the grays that softened all the harsh edges between them, listening to the silence of whirs and clicks and hums that electricity usually sent into the air.

Reveling in the quiet between them, the quiet that said more than any words could have expressed or explained.

Finally, after minutes? Hours? What did it matter? But finally the last of the crumbs were consumed, the last of the tea drunk and a chill started to invade their small space, because nothing lasted for ever.

Jordan moved first, picking up his dishes and hers, too, and putting them in the sink. "I'll light that fire now."

Using touch more than sight, Jordan knelt in front of the fireplace and struck a match to the logs he had laid earlier. The tinder caught, curling in on itself as the kindling took on the flame, then the bark on one of the larger logs started to burn until the fire swept under the whole triangle of wood, creating flames of blue to yellow at the tips.

He felt her come close then lean over his shoulder, putting her hand on his shoulder for support.

"Pretty." Her voice reflected the wonder of the ever-changing flames.

He only needed a quarter-turn of his head to bury his nose in her sweet-smelling hair. Instead, he stared straight ahead, trying to remember why he shouldn't touch, shouldn't taste.

"Yes." His thick throat produced a low, growling whisper. He should cough to clear it. But that would break the spell, wouldn't it?

Then again, he wasn't any woman's Prince Charming, was he? He could never be one of those men in the books Deseré read. He was just himself. A common man with a few truckloads of extra hang-ups...that he was trying to straighten out. He added that last thought like his therapist had told him to, cancelling out the negative with a positive.

The fire popped, startling Deseré so that she jumped back, lost her balance, tripped over his booted feet and ended up sprawled on her back on the rug, barely missing the coffee table.

He spun round, instinctively placing his hand across her belly as if he could keep her baby safe that way.

Her own hand lay over his, their fingers intermeshing.

The baby moved, sliding a hand or a foot from left to right, proving his existence under Jordan's hand.

And tears gathered in Jordan's eyes, tears he blinked to hide in the shadows of the flickering fire.

Tears that had too much emotion behind them to let them loose.

Tears that Deseré saw anyway.

"The miracle of life," she said softly as she sat up. "You can't help but be filled with emotion over something so mysteriously magnificent, can you?"

"Are you okay?"

"I'm fine." She shifted, gathering herself.

"Let me help you." Jordan reached around her, hugging her and pulling her close as he rose from his knees to his feet.

He'd been right that first day he'd seen her. Deseré's

head fit perfectly on his shoulder. Her body fit perfectly against his. Warmth greater than any fire lit him low in the the pit of his solar plexus.

It would be so easy to drop his head mere inches, to touch his lips to hers, to feel that flame leap between them.

It would be so easy.

And so wrong.

Because Deseré deserved more than what he could give her.

She deserved a mentally stable man who could hold her through the night without waking her from his fight with imaginary foes.

She deserved a financially stable man who could buy her fancy clothes from fancy stores instead of last year's leftovers from a feed store.

She deserved an emotionally stable man who didn't need to pay a professional to help him figure out what he felt and how to deal with those feelings.

Deseré deserved more than him.

With all his willpower, he looked down into her eyes, saw the question in them, and silently answered, in the negative.

Putting his hands on her shoulders to steady her, maybe to steady himself as well, he took a step back.

In the vaguely red-tinged light of the fireplace, he saw her face color in embarrassment.

"No," he said. "Don't."

She ducked her head, took her own step back and crossed her arms, tucking her hands in.

"Sorry." Her voice cracked.

"Me, too." He looked at the ceiling, trying to read any divine answers written there. But he only saw moving shadows. Ghosts that followed him wherever he went. "I can't have you."

She freed her hands to rub them up and down her arms. "Can you at least hold me? Just for tonight?"

His willpower broke. "Yes. Just for tonight."

Walking past him, brushing against him, she made her way to the couch. Sitting, she patted a place next to her. "Come sit with me."

He couldn't have told her no for all the gold in heaven.

He sat as far from her as he could, as if distance would create a barrier between them.

Drawing her knees up to her chin, she turned sideways to face him. "Aren't you lonely sometimes?"

He looked past her, trying to avoid the susceptibility in her face, sure it echoed his own. But he couldn't lie to her. Couldn't put her off with a shrug. He had to tell her the truth. "All the time."

Her smile drew his keen focus even though he fought it. It was a sad smile, delicate and fragile. "Me, too," she said.

He had to touch her, had to give her comfort.

He reached for her feet, covered in her oversize socks, and put them on his lap. He put his thumb against the arch of one foot, making slow, methodical circles against the thick wool.

Gracefully, she lay back, away from him, one arm flung over her head as she breathed out to let the rigidity of her body go. Still, the tension pulled and pushed between them, too strong to be so easily put to rest.

Distance. He needed distance.

"Tell me about your baby's father."

And the tension ratcheted up, not just between the two of them but between Deseré and the world.

Jordan wanted to stand guard over her and promise her he wouldn't let anyone hurt her ever again. But he couldn't do that. It wasn't his right.

And deep down, in that part of himself he tried to avoid exploring, he wasn't sure he could keep that promise anyway. Who was he to promise to keep anyone safe?

Instead, he just kept rubbing.

In the shifting shadows she said to the room at large, "I don't know who the father is."

Jordan's rubbing slowed, then picked up the rhythm again.

Deseré realized how that must sound. Should she let the words hang there, knowing he wouldn't ask anymore, or...?

"The baby is my sister's. In vitro. But she..."

Just say it, Deseré. Say it out loud and get it over with. "She died a few months ago in a car accident."

Her heart clenched as if a knife had just been thrust into it.

"She died. She died, she died, she died." Somewhere, in a distant part of her, she knew she kept repeating it over and over again.

She knew she had drawn herself up as tight as she could, arms and legs folded in as she rocked back and forth.

She knew that Jordan had shifted to pull her back against his chest as he sat sideways on the wide couch.

And she knew that it was Jordan's arms wrapped around her, keeping her from shattering into so many fractured pieces that she would have never been whole again.

For the first time since she'd answered the door to the two uniformed policemen who'd broken the news as carefully as they could, she had found a safe place to cry.

"Go ahead and cry, sweetheart. Cry as long as you need to. I've got you."

His deep voice in her ear broke through the last of her reserves.

How did he know? How could he have known that had been the perfect thing to say?

Everyone else, all those people at the hospital and at the funeral home who had hugged her, even though she hadn't wanted it, had tried to shush her, saying, "Don't cry. It will be all right," even though she hadn't even been crying at the time and she had known it would never be all right again.

Deseré let her emotions show, in the raw, with no holding back. She didn't think she could stop herself if she tried. But she knew that, safe in Jordan's arms, she didn't have to try. He had her, tightly. Securely. Safely. For as long as she needed him.

The fire had died down before her sobs turned to whimpers and still he held her.

The realization of what she'd just done, how she'd just let herself go, brought her back to herself and she sat up, pushing away from Jordan's emotionally and physically warm embrace.

Involuntarily, she shivered. She didn't have to do this. She didn't have to be strong alone.

"I need to put more logs on the fire," Jordan whispered in her ear. It was the same tone he'd used to tell her to go ahead and cry, that he would hold her until all her tears were spent.

"Don't go." That pleading tone was hers, left over from her childhood, with all her childhood fears behind it.

"I'll be right back," he promised.

"I believe you."

And when he crawled back in behind her and wrapped his arms around her once again, she leaned her head back and said, "I trust you."

He brushed his lips across her cheek, near her ear. "Thank you."

Though he left unsaid, *I trust you, too.* Why was that so important to her? She already had more than she would have dreamed of as she leaned against him, absorbing his strength.

Jordan thought she had drifted off into that half-sleep state when she shifted against him.

Quietly into the night, barely above the roar of the wind around them, she said, "This baby was never meant to be mine."

She faltered, as if waiting for encouragement from him. He didn't know what to do. What he wanted to do was to touch her face, touch her hair, *touch her soul as she was touching his.*

But he couldn't. This was a miracle moment between them. Deseré was made for a forever lifetime—and he wasn't.

Forevers were made up of responsibilities he couldn't handle.

He gave in to the impulse and pushed her hair from her cheek. His thumb came away damp.

Her tears tore at him.

He tried to speak. The words stuck in his throat.

But this was important to her. She needed to share her burdens and he was all she had.

He had to swallow twice, hard, to get his words out. "Why did you keep him, then?"

"At first, because he's a part of me. A part of my sister. He's all the family I have." She put her hand over her stomach. "And now—because I love him."

She lay so still he could hear her breathing. She gulped in air as if she needed the extra push, and sighed it out again in a rush.

Then she tensed, as if gathering herself together. He felt every muscle tighten, from neck through back to thighs and feet, as she lay on him.

"Relax, sweetheart. I've got you," he said, before he could stop himself. That was twice tonight. He clenched his jaw. What was he saying?

Then he made himself relax, too, to keep Deseré from feeding off his tension.

He must have been successful because she snuggled in deeper against him. "For all the years they were married, my sister Celeste gave up herself to be everything Santone told her to be.

"She helped him fool the world into thinking they were a perfect couple even though their marriage was never what my sister had hoped for. The illusion was important to Santone. He's very much into his public image.

"But it had a major flaw—they couldn't have children. He was sterile."

"Santone. This is Dr. Santone, who gave you a bad reference? The neurosurgeon on the board of the hospital you worked for?"

"That's the one."

"When I agreed to be their surrogate, Santone publicly explained it by blaming their fertility problems on my sister. I had the procedure done out of town so no one would know we used donor sperm instead of his sperm. Apparently, his self-esteem would have

suffered if his inner circle knew of his inability to pro-
create." Bitterness threaded through her tone, making
her voice harsh.

He hadn't known she could get any tenser, but she
did. Now she was so brittle he was afraid to touch her
in case she might break.

As if she'd read his mind, she threaded her fingers
through his.

Jordan squeezed her fingers. Knowing sympathy
would shut her down, he took a different tack and said
as sarcastically as he could, "Nice guy."

"Santone touted his progressiveness by telling everyone how we would all be the perfect family, me included. For a while Celeste was even able to convince
me to believe him." Deseré coughed up a hostile laugh.
"But Celeste helped Santone hide a lot more than fertility problems from the world and from me. I knew
Santone had a temper. Celeste denied that he'd ever
physically hurt her, but I have my doubts. What I don't
doubt is that Santone mentally tortured Celeste for all
the years they were married."

She let go of his hand to wipe a tear from her cheek
then immediately searched out his hand again, holding
on even tighter than before.

"My sister turned from an outgoing, outspoken,
brave woman to a compliant shadow who followed her
husband's orders without question."

Jordan sadly thought of a girl he'd gone to grade
school and high school with. "I've seen it happen."

He refused to think of his own relationship with his
father, an expert in mental abuse and physical abuse
as well. He hadn't turned meek and mild but had gone
the other way.

Wild, the town at large had all said. They'd all had

great sympathy for his parents when—his stomach clenched as he finished his thought—he'd killed Brad.

He'd had to leave town, had to leave behind the reminders everywhere he'd gone of the accident that should have never happened. If only…

But there were no such things as if-onlys.

"My sister always stood up for me."

So had his sister. She'd been the only one on his side. That's why he would do anything for her, including coming back to town to open the clinic.

"I would do anything for her." Deseré echoed his thoughts as she rubbed the baby that should have been her sister's. "I knew I was a point of contention between them, most probably because I urged my sister to stand up for herself." The crack in her voice told Jordan that Deseré might be second-guessing herself.

"You did the right thing."

She pulled the hand that was intertwined with hers over her belly, placing it so he could feel the baby move within her.

"I'm not sure why Santone agreed for me to become a surrogate for them. I have my suspicions it was to keep my sister in line. I don't know what happened—what changed. All I know is that Celeste was on the phone with me while on her way to the airport, crying, telling me she had to get away, when she ran the red light that killed her."

He let the silence fall as he honored her sister's memory with her. As he honored the memory of his best friend. As he grieved losses so deep he had been forever changed by them.

And he grieved that he could do nothing, give her nothing, promise her nothing to make her hurt go away.

She squeezed his hand, offering him comfort instead.

"I will always have a part of my sister in this baby she loved so deeply, even though she never knew him."

He squeezed back, feeling helpless and inadequate.

He untangled his fingers, pulling back and adjusting her off his lap, putting inches of distance between them.

Her eyes looked bruised in the shadows of the flickering fire.

What did his own look like? He turned away from her and shifted.

"It sounds like the wind has died down. I think I'll take a quick look around and then go on up to bed."

"In the dark? What if power lines are down?"

"I'll take a flashlight." He would take any risk to gain much-needed personal space between them.

"I've told you my deepest, darkest secrets, tell me yours. Tell me, Jordan, why everyone in this town talks about you in whispers." She grabbed for his hand but had to settle for covering his fist. "Please, stay."

If he were to open his palm, she might intertwine her fingers in his again and then he would have to stay, wouldn't he?

What to say? How to divert her? How to avoid a confession that would make Deseré want to get as far away from him as she could?

"Deseré, I—"

"Please, Jordan. You've given me comfort. Let me do the same for you." She picked up his hand and rubbed the back of it along her lips. The softness of her mouth emphasized the roughness of his hand. "It's what friends do. Share our burdens."

Was this his second chance? Could he tell her? Would she understand? Offer forgiveness he didn't deserve?

He took a breath, ready to speak, ready to—

In a startling, noisy instant all the lights came back

on, turning their cozy den into an overly bright interrogation room. Motors began to run as the central-heating fan whirred and the refrigerator rumbled. Life as he knew it returned to normal.

Gently, he sat up, raising Deseré with him.

Still, she clung to him. "Tell me."

But her eyes reflected what they both knew.

The moment had been lost.

And for him there was no forgiveness, no second chances, no new, innocent life to fill the hole in his soul.

He untwined their fingers, putting her hands in her lap, and stood. "I'm going to take a look around to see if there's any obvious damage."

As he grabbed his flashlight and stepped outside, he thought he would feel grateful that he had avoided revealing his own damaged self.

Instead, he felt more isolated and alone than he had since that day so long ago when he'd woken up in the hospital and his father had told him that his best friend was dead and it was all his fault.

CHAPTER ELEVEN

DESERÉ FELT LIKE she'd just been pushed out into the cold.

What had happened?

She'd thought they had finally breached that wall between them. In fact, she was sure of it.

But then the lights had come on and she'd found she had been so wrong. Jordan's eyes had been flat, his face drained of all emotion. His movements stiff and unyielding, like he'd had to keep his shoulders braced for an onslaught.

Was that what he'd thought of her questions? Of her concern? That she had been bombarding him through curiosity instead of trying to comfort him with compassion?

Rubbing her hands over the chill bumps on her arms, she stood, refusing to wait for him when he obviously didn't want her to.

Instead, she took herself to bed. Normally, she would have stayed awake, replaying those last few minutes of conversation over and over in her head, assuring herself she hadn't read them wrong. He had felt close to her. He had been about to open up. He had been about to share, sealing the bond between them.

And there was a bond. Of that she had no doubt.

But baby James took care of putting her to sleep as exhaustion dragged her down into a deep and dreamless rest when morning came too soon with the ringing of her alarm clock and soft morning sunshine beaming through her half-open curtains.

Coming face to face with Jordan was a certainty. What would she do? What would she say?

She still didn't know as she walked down the stairs to smell breakfast cooking.

Kitchen noise, which normally comforted her, jangled her nerves.

He had the table set for two. Omelets, her favorite, were on plates kept warm on the stove. A glass of milk and a cup of hot tea sat next to her plate.

Although she'd been greeted with plenty of breakfasts just like this one, this morning seemed very different, as if he was putting special effort into it.

But, then, last night had felt the same.

"Good morning." His voice flat and emotionless, he didn't look at her as he said it, his attention focused on the omelet in the pan instead.

Having shown a smidgeon of vulnerability, now Jordan was pulling more into himself than he'd ever been. She recognized the tendency in herself.

But what they had between them was too much to let it go—as if letting go was even an option for her anymore.

She loved him. It was both that simple and that complex. She had to try. "About last night—"

He turned to her, interrupting. "Are you okay?"

"Yes. Are you?"

He turned away. "Yeah, sure. I'm fine."

He dropped the spatula in the sink. It clattered, jangling her nerves.

"I've got things to do today. Let me know if you need anything before I leave and I'll add it to the list," he said, but his tone didn't encourage her.

"I need to know more about you."

He shook his head. "Let it go."

"Just like that? No more friendship?"

The cords in his neck tightened. "There are better people in town to be friends with."

He turned to her, his face blank. But his eyes showed her a fleeting moment of sadness. "Let's eat."

Her stomach clenched at the thought of food, at the idea of sitting across from him as he pulled back from her further with every bite she took. As she watched him build walls around himself to keep her out.

"I've got to go myself. Don't want to be late. The boss has a thing about that." Her laugh sounded painful, like a broken branch scraping down a tin roof.

She would have to walk past him to get her purse and keys. Being that close to him, breathing in his scent, feeling the heat from his body, feeling that undefinable presence that set her nerve endings tingling and her heart on fire, would be the details that had her throwing herself into his arms, seeking his strength, his protection, his love.

Futility made every breath heavy to draw in and release as if the air held no life-sustaining energy for her.

"You've got to eat." Even as he issued it as an order, his concern came through.

Damn it. Why couldn't he be an overbearing jerk? That would make all this so much easier.

She shook her head. "No appetite."

"I'll wrap your breakfast up for you."

"No. I don't need you to do anything for me. Just like you don't need me doing anything for you." And those words made her armor drop solidly into place. *Survive, Deseré. Keep yourself safe and survive.*

It had been a while since Celeste had invaded her thoughts, but now her sister was first and foremost in her head. *He's a man, honey. And men can't be trusted.*

She found the fortitude to brush by him to grab her purse and keys.

If he had reached for her, even shifted his weight in her direction, she would have stopped, turned and lost her resolve.

But he didn't. He actually shifted farther away from her. The warmth she always felt around him wasn't there. In its place was a cold pulling in, a severing of that connection that had built so slowly she hadn't even noticed it was there until now.

The void made her knees feel weak. Worse, it made her heart feel empty.

Before he could see the tears gathering in her eyes she pushed her way out the door and down the steps.

By the time she slid into her car, she had forcibly pushed their whole night's conversation into a box she would avoid opening at all costs.

As she unlocked the door to the clinic, she had a plan. Pretend this had never happened.

"I'm glad you're here early," Nancy said in way of greeting. "You've got a full schedule."

"Good. Glad to hear it." Finally, she was catching a break. Keeping herself busy would keep her mind off Jordan and the conversation they weren't going to have.

As she slipped on her lab coat, she also slipped on the professionalism she'd worked so hard to obtain. The professionalism and self-respect and independence no man would take from her.

But he'd never tried to take any of those things from, her wayward subconscious said. In fact, Jordan had done everything in his power to build her reputation—except for the living-together part. And that part was worth a whisper or two behind her back.

Or it had been until last night. This morning's coldness—no, it was worse than coldness, it was nothingness—would make living with Jordan very empty with a hole in her soul that ached to be filled. How long could she withstand that kind of pain?

She didn't make enough money to move out. What would she do?

She had no choice but to keep on doing what she'd been doing, sharing living space with him. She would keep to herself, stay in her room, become a ghost in his house.

Not the best solution, but the only one she had right now.

Nancy handed her the first chart. "Regina Taylor. She's missed her period but has been on the Pill. She says she been consistent but she's only sixteen. How many of us are consistent at sixteen?" Nancy glanced down at Deseré's stomach. "Or at any age?"

Nancy's look held so many questions. What did Nancy think of her? What did the whole town, the town where she would be raising her son, think of her?

As she pushed the door open she decided she couldn't dwell on that now. Instead, she plastered on her professional face and entered the room. "Regina, how are you feeling today?"

This is how she would survive. Burying herself in her job then in her son. It had been enough before Jordan. It would be enough now, too.

She smiled past the pain in her heart. For her patient's sake. For baby James's sake. For her own sake. She would survive.

CHAPTER TWELVE

Sitting in his truck with the radio playing soft and low, Jordan waited outside the clinic, watching for Deseré to lock the door behind her and head toward her car. After his therapy session he felt raw and exposed. Vulnerable. He could so easily be hurt.

But he would survive it. His therapist and he had talked about that so many times in the past. He had never had a reason to risk it, though, risk the pain that came with misunderstanding or rejection.

Finally, he saw the overhead lights flick off, with only the safety lights leaving a glow inside the building.

He saw Deseré. His heart jumped then plunged.

This could go wrong, terribly wrong. Then what would happen? They lived together. They had little choice.

But they couldn't keep living together with all he had bottled up inside him.

So he had no choice.

He opened the door to his truck.

She looked up, wariness on her face.

"Hi." His throat felt tight and hot. He worked hard to keep from clenching his jaw but he couldn't manage the conciliatory expression he wanted to offer her.

All he could offer was open and honest desperation and yearning.

She froze and stared at him. Whatever she saw made her thaw, at least enough to give him a half-smile. "Hi."

"Take a drive with me?"

She looked back at her car, as if looking for an escape route before she turned back and said, "Okay."

He held out his keys. After what he had to tell her, she would feel more secure if she drove.

And, he admitted to himself, he didn't trust himself to drive responsibly if the conversation went where he intended it to go.

She took them, careful to touch only the key ring and not his hand. "Okay."

He opened the door for her and held out his hand to help her into the driver's seat.

Heat passed between them, so much heat he felt the need to wipe off her burning touch. But then he would feel cold again, wouldn't he?

He didn't say anything other than to direct her out of town toward the two-lane highway in the opposite direction of the ranch.

She bit her lip as she drove but kept her silence, too.

Yes, they meshed. Just like the natural way their fingers intertwined, their spirits intertwined, too.

Casually, tentatively, he put his hand out, palm open, on the console armrest that separated them.

Without looking at him, he felt her hand slide onto his, bridging the gap. Palm to palm, her fingertips resting on his, her touch gave him the courage he needed.

"Wild and out of control. That's how my teachers described me when I hit my teens. The ones who knew me from middle school didn't know what happened. I'd always been quiet, almost invisible before then. I liked to read. I liked spending time at the ranch with the horses." He laughed, but it sounded more like a bubble of pain bursting than a bubble of happiness.

"My father always had visitors out to the ranch and he expected me to make an impression on them but the ranch was big enough that I could usually escape that. My favorite days were spent mucking out the stalls, working with the foals, then finding a corner in a quiet loft and reading until someone found me. Plato made sure to never find me until it was time to go home."

Softly, she asked, "What changed?"

"Having quiet, shy offspring didn't suit Dean Hart. As his firstborn and only son, I was supposed to make my mark on the town, on the world. My sister was doing it. She was head cheerleader. President of her class. Always hanging with the popular kids. She led volunteer groups and always knew how to brighten up a room. And she was younger than me. If she could do it, why couldn't I?

"So I tried. I dated the popular girls, whether I wanted to or not. Of course, they didn't turn down Dean Hart's son, even if I wasn't their ideal date. I played football and didn't do half-badly, even though I hated it. Made friends with Brad, who was all the things my father wanted me to be, except in a wild way instead of a socially acceptable way. It was the best I could do."

When he fell silent, Deseré nudged him by asking, "How was school?"

"Before high school I had always made good grades. Drinking hard, partying all night and skipping class to sleep off my hangovers made keeping up my school work impossible. The drinking was probably the key to it all. But I couldn't be outgoing without it.

"So, the more I disappointed my father, the harder I

tried to get it right, which meant I drank more. My teen years were not my best."

"What happened?" Deseré had no judgment in her tone. Maybe, Jordan hoped, he even heard understanding and compassion there.

"I flunked my college entrance exams." He blinked, realizing how far they had come. "Turn onto the next road. It's a small single-lane dirt road and not well marked, so you'll have to slow down to not miss it."

She nodded to indicate she'd heard him.

He swallowed to push down the lump that would keep the rest of his confession from coming out. "I was too hungover from celebrating winning the big game the night before to concentrate on the four-hour test."

She tightened her threaded fingers on his fingers, making an anchor there when his memories made him feel as if he might go spinning off the edge of the universe.

"Totally flunked?" she asked, as if she knew he had overstated his failure. Her faith in him made him less empty inside.

"A far as my father went, I flunked. In truth, I had made a high enough score to get into a state college but not good enough to get me into A&M, where my father wanted me to go. There was a fight, of course. All the usual things were said. How I was stupid and a disgrace and he could hardly believe I was a Hart."

"What did you say to him?"

The question surprised him. "Nothing. I never said anything. It wouldn't have done any good and would have only prolonged the lecture." He pointed ahead. "Turn in there."

She slowed, putting on her blinker to turn onto the road that was barely a path cut into the woods.

"This once led to an active oil field. My father had a partnership in the company that drilled. It was shut down about the time I was born, I think."

"Not that you're to blame for the oilfield running dry, right?" She said it lightly but with a touch of seriousness beneath her question.

"Not to hear my father talk about it. According to him, I'm responsible for everything bad that has ever happened to his family."

"His family. Not your family?"

He shook his head, trying to shake off the sense of loss. "Not my family. Not anymore. It's better that way." He blinked, getting his bearings. "You'll come to a hairpin curve in a moment. When you do, stop there, okay?"

"Okay." She let stillness fall between them just long enough for him to start retreating into himself before she asked, "Then what happened?", calling him back to her.

He took a breath and readied himself to finish it.

"When my grades came in and every college my father wanted me to attend had turned me down, he said…" The pain of his father's words struck him silent. He skipped to the part he could say aloud. "So Brad and I raided both our parents' stashes of alcohol then drove my truck as fast as it would go. We ended up on this dirt road leading to nowhere, running from nothing and everything."

Jordan realized they weren't moving. Deseré had stopped at the curve, the one with the big ditch and the scarred, skeletal, dead oak tree on the other side of it. How had she known?

"This is where the truck left the road and ended upside down there." He pointed to the ditch he had visited too many times. "I wound up with a concussion."

Deseré wiped the tears from her cheeks as she stared at the place his best friend had lost his life and he had lost his soul.

And now, after all these years of keeping quiet, he couldn't keep it in anymore. "No one could say for sure who'd been driving and I don't remember.

"I was thrown clear. Brad didn't have as much luck.

"All I remember is that the white walls of the hospital seemed to close in on me and I wondered if Brad had felt as trapped in his coffin as I did in my hospital bed."

Now Deseré wiped the tears from his cheeks. Her soft, strong hand smelled of lotion. He kissed her fingertips as she rubbed them across his lips.

"I wasn't allowed to attend the funeral. His parents didn't want me there. Two weeks later I joined the army and took myself out of their sight so they could try to heal."

Deseré untangled her hand from his. He clenched it into a fist to keep from reaching for her.

But then she opened the door of the truck and slid out. Coming around to his door, she opened it for him and held her hand out. "Come on."

He reached for her, holding on too tightly, but she didn't protest. Instead, she led him to the side of the road, to the ditch where Brad had died.

She cleared her throat and looked up at the sky. "You were a good friend when Jordan needed one. Thank you, Brad. He's sorry and he misses you and he'll never forget you."

She said the words he'd always wanted to say, the words he'd never thought he had a right to say.

Huge gulps of pain rushed through him, making him shake. She pulled his arm over her shoulder, steadying him.

As a breeze swayed the tall grasses she touched his face, making sure he was listening.

"Do you hear that?" she whispered.

The wind was making the grasses swish. It was a fragile, gentle sound, very clean and pure.

"I hear it." The sound felt like the subtle brush against his soul he had lived so long without.

"Brad says he forgives you." She put her hand on his cheek, to comfort and to keep him from turning away. "Now it's time you forgave yourself."

For the first time Jordan thought that someday he might be able to.

CHAPTER THIRTEEN

AND JORDAN DID his typical pulling away from her.

After a week of living with a man who was no more than a warm body—make that a cold spirit—Deseré broke down and talked to Nancy.

"What should I do?"

"Jordan's never had it easy. Not with that father of his." Nancy picked up a file and put it down again. "There were rumors that Dean Hart thought Jordan wasn't his. Maybe that's why he was so hard on his son. But Jordan could do nothing right—while his sister could do nothing wrong."

"Was it always like that?"

Nancy nodded. "My daughter and he were in the same classes. Jordan was a quiet kind of boy. Very bright. He never had to study, just got it the first time, whatever subject he was learning. And he was interested in everything. I used to volunteer in the school library. Jordan read everything he could get his hands on."

"He still does." Those many hours she and Jordan spent reading in easy company were some of the best of her life.

"But being smart wasn't good enough for his father. Dean wanted Jordan to be popular, to be outgoing, to be the life of the party. After all, his sister was."

Nancy clasped her hands together. "Jordan would come to school with bruises. No one had the courage to ask him about them. I'm not sure he would have told anyone anything anyway. What good would it have done? No one stood up to Dean Hart."

"What about his mother?"

"Least of all her. She wouldn't risk the lifestyle she enjoyed. Shopping trips to Dallas kept her in line."

"Did his father beat his sister, too?"

"I don't think so. It seems Dean only treated his son poorly."

"We were making progress. So much progress. But now... It's like we've reached a limit and now we're sliding backward." Helplessness made Deseré's heart sink. "What can I do?"

Nancy shook her head. "I don't know. Have patience. Show compassion. The same things you do here in the office but on a more personal scale."

On a more personal scale. Everything about Jordan was personal to her.

"How do I do that?"

Outside, Jordan's truck rumbled into the parking lot. He got out, stopping to give his leftover lunch to a dog that had recently begun to hang around the clinic. Slowly, cautiously, to keep from spooking the dog, Jordan held out his hand but the dog turned and ran for a few feet before stopping to look over his shoulder.

Jordan stayed still until the dog turned to face him fully.

When the dog showed trust, Jordan rewarded him by putting a bite of hamburger on the ground then backing away so the dog could eat in peace. While Deseré couldn't hear Jordan's words, she was sure he was speaking quietly and encouragingly to the animal. The same way you would gentle an injured wild animal.

So for the next days and weeks Deseré spoke quietly, rewarded with smiles and encouraging words.

And little by little Jordan responded.

When she walked past him she would let her hand casually brush him. He no longer jerked away, and once or twice she was certain he leaned into it. And maybe, just maybe, he was choosing to cross paths with her for that touch between them, that electric touch that always produced tingles.

And he would do things to make her smile. He bought her a pregnancy T-shirt that had a tiny cowboy on a rocking horse on it.

"Chin up," he said when he handed her the shirt that blatantly announced her pregnancy.

"Chin up," she agreed. And he didn't pull away when she rested her hand on his arm.

At Thanksgiving dinner, surrounded by his cousin Rusty, Rusty's girlfriend and his maternal aunt and uncle, he actually laughed. And later, as he helped her from his truck, he reached out for her hand, held it longer than necessary then gave her a quick hug and a thank-you for making this holiday a good one.

He was trying. Really trying. But now, with his barriers breached, the pain felt like a constant bruise.

In his head he knew he was going through change and change took time. His self-image fluctuated between who he wanted to be and who he thought he was, keeping him off balance.

Deseré held him steady through it all, ignoring his short-temperedness and lapses into silence, welcoming his conversation when he could find the will to communicate.

He did his best to show her how much he appreciated her strength, how much he valued her presence, how much he wanted to be a man she could be proud of.

The week before Christmas they hung the border in the baby's room, pastel cowboy hats and boots. She had insisted he look through the limited selection available at the feed store with her and when he'd mentioned he liked it, she had declared it perfect. And when he'd brought down his old rocking horse from the attic, she had cried.

It had been a good moment as she had chattered about cribs and curtains until she'd started asking him questions about his childhood holidays.

Which was why now, two days before Christmas, he was carrying a sappy, sticky cedar tree over his shoulder as he entered the house.

Jordan hauled in the Christmas tree he'd bought as an apology to Deseré, hoping to make up for the hurt he'd seen in her eyes when he'd snapped at her that he didn't want to talk about holiday memories.

She'd mentioned it casually, talking about the oyster stuffing her mother had made compared to the cornbread dressing his aunt made. And when he'd said he usually spent Christmas Day catching up on end-of-year paperwork, she'd given him a sad, pitying smile.

He didn't need that. Didn't want that. Didn't need…

He'd been trying, really trying.

But need led to weakness. Need was a weapon to be exploited.

As he and his therapist had discussed, Jordan stopped himself from thinking those same old thoughts. Deseré had never hurt him, had never tried to hurt him. Deseré trusted him.

And he could trust her.

He wanted to be the man she needed him to be—like she was the woman he needed her to be. He wanted to have a future with Deseré.

All the hard head work he'd been doing was worth it when Deseré saw the tree and the box of decorations he'd picked up at the feed store.

As she hung the lower ornaments and directed him to hang the higher ones, Jordan felt like this was his first Christmas ever.

They drank hot chocolate while Ebenezer Scrooge did his thing on the television that played softly in the background.

"What do you want for Christmas?" she asked him.

He was nonplussed. How could he tell her he already had more than he could have ever expected?

So he shrugged and turned the question back to her. "What do you want?"

"You." She said it matter-of-factly. "All of you, heart, mind, body and soul.'

I want you, too, he thought back at her. But he couldn't say it, no matter how hard he tried.

After a few moments of silence she touched his arm, gave him a tremulous smile then walked away, with a big sigh echoing in her wake.

That sigh breeched his last barrier as no push or shout could have. Need engulfed him, need to make her world better. Need to give her what she wanted. Need to give him what he wanted, too.

A peacefulness settled deep inside him. Next time, and he knew there would be a next time, with Deseré there always was—next time would be different, better. Because he would be different. Better. The best he could be for her and baby James.

That night Deseré came to him, waking him from his dreams.

Her head nestled into his chest and he felt as if he was the one giving comfort instead of her. He felt very strong, very protective and very much her man.

She made snuffling, snuggling noises against his chest, noises that made both his mind and his body beg to hear what sounds she would make when they made love.

"Jordan," she whispered in the moonlight, "if you want to…"

She ducked her head back shyly as she ran a single finger down his chest, making his heart throb. That throb circulated through his whole body, coming to a peak deep and low in his solar plexus.

"I want to." His hand reached out, catching her wandering finger and bringing it to his mouth.

She ran her foot up his shin, making him tremble. "I want to, too."

He put his lips on her smooth, bare shoulder, where her oversize T-shirt fell away, and kissed up her neck, tasting the sweetness of her delicate skin.

He ran his hand down her spine, tracing the outline of that feminine backbone that kept him together when he needed her most. How could she be so soft yet so resilient at the same time?

"Saying no to you is the hardest thing I've ever done, Deseré." Using all his willpower, he commanded his hand to stop midway when all he wanted to do was cup her delicious bottom in his hand and puller her closer, protecting baby James between them.

"I want to make love to you more than anything in the world. But this is about more than me and you, Deseré. This is about James, too." He put his hand on her belly, feeling a tiny foot or maybe a hand move under his palm. "A child needs a steady father. A father he can count on. A father who will always be there for him, no matter what he does, no matter how he screws up. A father who will love him for exactly who he is and not with any preconceived ideas about who he should be."

Deseré sat up, dislodging Jordan's hand. "There are plenty of children who do just fine without a father like that."

"But James doesn't have to. I can be the kind of father who loves unconditionally. I know this because I already love your son that way."

He took a deep breath, continuing despite the tension he felt in Deseré. "The steadiness? I'm working on that part. Working on finding my balance, on being okay with who I am, on living up to my own expectations and not my father's. I'm learning that I can't please him and I have to be okay with that."

She covered his hand, which rested on her belly, and squeezed his fingers. "I know. I'm very proud of you for that, too."

"But always being there?" He pinned her with a look that seemed to try to see into her soul. "That's up to you. Will you allow me to be a father to your son? Will you allow me to be your husband?"

She needed more than for Jordan to marry her for her son. That's what his father had done for his mother and it hadn't made for a good marriage. That's what Santone had wanted to do with her.

Jordan wasn't Santone, far from it, but she wasn't his mother or her sister, either.

"You're a good man, Jordan Hart, but I'll only marry for love."

Deseré waited for the three little words that would complete them all.

He let out a sigh as he stared at the ceiling, absently tracing the outline of James's foot.

Just as she was drifting off to sleep she thought she heard Jordan whisper, "I love you, Deseré."

When she looked over, his eyes were closed and his breathing was deep and even.

Christmas Eve. It was going to be a long day.

Jordan headed to the ranch before Deseré stirred.

When he pulled up in his truck, Rusty came out of the barn to meet him, looking grim. "The buyer will be out late this afternoon to pick her up."

Jordan nodded. He was doing the right thing. Just because it hurt like hell didn't change that.

He walked into the barn and Valkyrie gave him a welcome whinny.

"It will be okay, girl. You're going to a good owner who will treat you right."

She nudged him and he scratched that place behind her left ear that made her give him dreamy horse eyes.

"It's got to be done. I can't think of any other way."

As if she understood, she nodded under his palm then nibbled the front of his shirt.

Turning away from her wasn't as hard as it had been to turn away from Deseré last night, but it was close.

With nothing but a backward wave at Rusty, Jordan climbed into his truck and headed for the clinic.

That morning, when Deseré came down for breakfast, she saw that Jordan had plugged in the tree lights for her.

It was the little things that showed her they were making progress and that encouraged her to be patient.

Just as she was trying to be patient about the arrival of baby James. Just a few more weeks, her doctor had said at her last check-up. Mid-January.

The Braxton-Hicks contraction reminded Deseré to call the billing department of the hospital to find out why her last check hadn't cleared.

With an office full of people, finding a private moment had been impossible until now.

She looked up as the judge and Plato laughed, as old men did.

Plato had come in earlier to have his vitals checked so he could get a refill on his high blood pressure medicine and the judge had come for a refill for his Viagra, which he now clutched in a brown paper bag.

The joy in the old men's voices made her smile, too, despite what the accountant on the phone was telling her for the second time.

She listened as the accounts manager thoroughly and slowly explained that the hospital hadn't cashed the last check because Deseré's account had been paid in full last week. They had put the check in the mail yesterday to mail it back to her.

"Who paid it?" The hang-up phone calls she'd been getting more frequently came to mind. Sinister chills ran down her spine.

"I don't know. Santa? It was paid in cash," the man on the end of the line said. "Merry Christmas."

Just as her belly gave her the slightest cramp, Jordan came into the office. He'd been doing that for the last several weeks, coming in on his days off, taking the load off her.

She had wanted to suggest he reduce her paycheck but couldn't figure out how to pay ahead on the hospital bill if she did. And now it seemed she didn't need to worry about it.

But she was now worried for a different reason than money.

Was this paid hospital bill the work of Santone? Another way to claim he owned the baby she was carrying? That he owned her, too?

"Hey," Jordan said to her softly. "Are you feeling okay?"

She was achy all over and hormonal—which meant aching for Jordan's touch, aching for him to give her some release. Eight and a half months of being sexually on the edge would tend to make a woman a little testy, wouldn't it?

Add to that emotional state her tender feelings for Jordan, which he pushed away, and she was a hot mess.

She would like to blame it all on hormones but she had a feeling of dread that none of this would go away just because she gave birth.

The only way to get away from all her tumultuous feelings was to leave here, leave Jordan. And that made her feel more upset than any of the other emotions she was experiencing.

As the office got quiet, she realized she was listening to a dead phone line.

All the men were looking at the two strangers who had just pulled open the door, two strangers who stood there, staring at her.

But, then, one on them wasn't a stranger to her at all.

"Santone." She dropped the phone receiver. It clattered on the counter.

"Deseré." He took a step toward her but Jordan put himself between them.

Santone frowned. "If you'll excuse me, I'm here to talk to the mother of my child."

Jordan glared at him as if he were a bug he was about to squash then turned his attention to the other man. "And you are?"

The smaller man held out his hand with a card in it. Jordan took it.

"David Kessler. Life insurance agent."

"And your business?"

"I think Ms. Novak, Mr. Santone and I could use some privacy."

Deseré stayed behind the counter, feeling very safe with Jordan in front of her. "I'm among friends. We can talk about anything here."

The insurance agent looked worried then nodded. "I'm here to award the proceeds of Mrs. Celeste Santone's life insurance policy to Mr. Santone as the parent of her child. We just need your verification that your role is solely as surrogate."

He dug a sheaf of papers from his briefcase. "If you would sign this affidavit stating that Mr. Santone is the child's father and will be taking custody of the baby once it is born. There is a secondary policy payout you will receive once you verify you're the surrogate."

Deseré rubbed her back where baby James lay heavily on her kidney. "This is my child and he—" her hand quivered as she pointed at Santone "—is not my baby's father."

"Or course I am." Santone took a step forward but stopped when Jordan moved toward him.

Jordan looked from Santone back to Deseré with a look that was both hesitant and wistful.

At Deseré's nod, he looked the insurance agent straight in the face. "I'm the child's father and Deseré is the child's mother."

"You're not." Santone's tone was so menacing, both Plato and the judge rose to their feet.

Quietly, Jordan asked, "I suggest you calm yourself in front of my fiancé. Would you like to do a blood test to prove your paternity after the baby's born?"

The insurance agent gave a deep sigh. "This is rather complicated, isn't it?"

The judge spoke up. "What would make it clearer for you, young man?"

The agent glanced down at the papers he carried. "The way the policy is written, if I can show that Ms. Novak isn't dependent on Mr. Santone for any of the expenses for the child, I can say she is not a surrogate but the child's mother."

The conversation she just had with the hospital made her feel light-headed. Had Santone paid that bill?

The judge asked, "Like what expenses?"

"Food. Shelter. Clothing. Hospital bills."

Jordan cleared his throat. "Either Deseré or I have paid for all those."

"Can you prove it?"

He nodded. "I have accounts at the grocery store and the feed store." His half-smile was crooked and embarrassed. "The feed store is where we've been purchasing maternity clothes."

"And medical bills?"

Deseré pulled her purse from under the counter and started going through receipts. "Here."

She thrust the crumpled receipts at the agent.

Jordan reached into his wallet and pulled out a folded receipt, too. "And this is from the hospital where I've prepaid for our son's delivery."

Our son. Pride clogged Jordan's throat as he said that. His son. Deseré had given him that privilege.

"So you claim paternity, Mr....?"

"Dr. Hart." He pulled his driver's license from his wallet and handed it to the agent. "Dr. Jordan Hart."

The agent checked the license and handed it back then cleared his throat.

To the room at large, he said, "The policy beneficiaries are listed as the parents and guardians of Mrs. Celeste Santone's child. Are you telling me that the child you are carrying, Ms. Novak, belongs to you and Dr. Hart?"

"Yes. He's our baby. Mine and Jordan's."

The world around Jordan seemed to pulse with a whole different light as joy burst so big inside him he felt every cell fill with incredible happiness.

He hadn't known, or even suspected, that love could feel this big.

"You lie. This man is not the father." Santone surged forward but again Jordan blocked his path to Deseré.

The agent sucked in his cheeks. "Your only option at this point, Dr. Santone, is to wait until the child is born and submit to a DNA test."

The judge picked up his cellphone and held it so Santone could see it. "Seems to me your business is done here. Do I need to call my boys with badges to escort you out of town?"

Santone shifted from foot to foot before he glared at them all and stalked out of the clinic.

As quickly as he could, Jordan went to Deseré's side, putting his arm around her in support. Calmness settled over him as she leaned against him, accepting what he offered.

Nancy walked in from the back. "Our last patient just called and cancelled her appointment. Looks like we get to leave extra-early today. I think I'll go home and take a nap."

The judge and Plato both put on their coats and picked up their hats.

"Sounds like a good plan to me," the judge said as he shook his paper bag. "Merry Christmas, ya'll."

Jordan turned to Deseré. "A nap sounds like a good plan for you, too."

"For us, you mean?" Deseré challenged him.

Before he could answer, Nancy glanced at the two of them. "Go ahead. I'll lock up."

Deseré made her way to Jordan's truck, appreciating that he opened the door for her and helped her in. The step up into the cab took more effort on his part as he lifted her under both elbows to help her lift her baby bump inside. Why did she feel so much heavier today? She would have to pay more attention to her salt intake.

After he helped her with her seat belt and then started up the truck she said, "For a man who doesn't like to talk much, you had a lot to say back there."

He turned his focus to her, his eyes bright and sparkly with a hint of wariness in them, his lips lifting in the corners as if he'd just eaten a smile as he just said, "Hmmph."

"Hmmph is right." She crossed her arms, propping them on her stomach as she didn't have anywhere else to put them. "I don't know where to start."

Obligingly, Jordan turned down the radio that had begun to blare out a commercial for custom-made horse trailers and waited.

"Did you pay my hospital bills?"

"Yes." He stopped at a four-way stop sign but didn't move forward, even though no other cars were coming.

"Want to expound on that?"

"Not really."

She blew out a breath. "Do it for me anyway, okay?"

He blew out a breath, too. "Okay."

He put the truck into park, right there in the middle

of the road. But, then, it was unlikely the big town of Piney Woods would suddenly develop a traffic problem.

He opened his mouth, closed it again and swallowed.

Deseré knew the pattern. Mentally, she counted to four and, as she expected, he started talking.

"I wanted to."

"How? I know your finances as well as I know mine and our last few months have been slow."

"I sold Valkyrie." His voice cracked when he confessed it.

"You *what*?" Another contraction grabbed her, this time strong enough to make her catch her breath.

"It had to be done." He gripped the steering-wheel. "I want to take care of you, Deseré. You and the baby. It makes me feel good."

"I don't know what to say."

"You don't need to say anything."

"Thank you. It's not enough—but thank you. You have all my gratitude."

"I don't expect thanks or gratitude." Jordan rubbed his hand over his face. "I meant it when I said I want to be part of James's life."

"Is Valkyrie gone already?"

He shook his head. "The new owner is picking her up this afternoon. She's a Christmas gift."

"Could we drive out so I can say goodbye?"

"Yes, we can do that." Jordan put the truck back into gear and head for the ranch, realizing as he did so that having Deseré by his side as Valkyrie was trailered away would make the pain more bearable.

CHAPTER FOURTEEN

BY THE TIME they got to the ranch Deseré had to work hard to keep from squirming. Not only did she not have enough room but every time she moved, the seat belt tightened up, putting more and more pressure against her hard belly.

Rusty greeted them as they rolled to a stop.

As Jordan climbed out of the truck Rusty asked in a loud whisper, "Everything okay?"

Did he really think she couldn't hear him?

Jordan shrugged away his cousin's question. "Deseré came to see Valkyrie."

Again that stage whisper. "So you told her, huh?"

"Yes, he told me." She winced as her crankiness came through. But her back was beginning to ache and she had really wanted time alone with Jordan without Rusty to overhear.

Jordan came round and opened the door, handing her down as gracefully as the two of them could manage.

Rusty whistled. "Getting big there, huh, Deseré?"

Before Deseré could respond to that, Jordan gave him a hard stare. "I'm sure you have something to do that's not here, right?"

"Maybe I should check the oil levels on the tractor."

"Good idea."

And just like that, Deseré had what she wanted. Time alone with Jordan.

"Sun feels good, doesn't it?" He looked up at the sky full of cotton-ball clouds. "Typical Texas December day, warm and barely breezy. Shirtsleeve weather. It could turn cold and snow tomorrow, though."

"Weather talk always means you're avoiding something."

"Let's go and say hello to Valkyrie."

"Hello and goodbye." Deseré wanted to thank him again, to apologize for being the cause of his sacrifice, to make him feel better, but whatever she said would likely have the wrong results.

Male ego. Such a fragile and complex thing.

He held onto her elbow as she walked toward the barn.

"Hey, pretty girl." Deseré held out her hand and Valkyrie nuzzled it. "Thank you for doing this for me and for baby James." She sent a sideways glance at Jordan and was relieved to see he was nodding along with Valkyrie. He wasn't looking at the mare, though. He was looking at her.

Now was the time.

"Jordan?"

"Hmm?"

"Why did you tell them we were engaged?"

Jordan turned back to the stall, resting his boot on the lowest wooden rail of the stall. "Because I wanted it to be true."

"You want to marry me?"

"Um-hmm."

"Why?"

"The usual reasons."

"Could you give me a little more detail?"

"Because…" He took his foot off the bottom slat. "Because I want to be a good father to James. I want to take care of both of you. I want to hold you in my arms every night after we have sex."

"Wild and out-of-control sex?"

"If that's the way you want it."

"On Tuesdays and Fridays. But sweet, gentle sex on Mondays and Wednesdays and marathon sex on Saturdays."

"And on Sundays?"

"Potluck."

He seemed to be considering it. Finally he said, "I can do that."

She smiled at him. "I know you can."

He turned back to stare past Valkyrie. Deseré thought about letting her last question drop. But, no, she needed to hear it.

"Jordan?"

"Hmm?"

"Any other reason you want to marry me?"

This time, when he turned to face her, he put both his hands on her shoulders and looked straight into her eyes. In those dark, tender depths she saw the answer she was looking for.

She didn't have to wait that long before he said, in a deep rich voice, "I love you."

She let out the breath she hadn't realized she had been holding. "I love you, too, you know."

"I was hoping you'd say that."

"Then, yes." She shifted, too anxious to stand still.

"Yes?"

"Yes, I'll marry you."

He stood frozen, as if he was replaying their conversation in his head. She counted, one, two, three, four.

"I'd like that as soon as possible."

"But first…"

"Yeah?"

"I think you may need to deliver our baby."

Panic closed off every thought Jordan had.

"Are you sure?" he managed to put enough words together in order to ask.

"Pretty sure." She put his hand against her contracting belly. "I haven't timed them but they're getting stronger."

"When did they start?"

"This morning in the shower, but I thought they were Braxton-Hicks ones and ignored them."

Jordan glanced at his watch and noted the time while he guided her toward the tack room. "I'll blow up the air mattress."

"That would be nice." She grimaced as she said it. "Hey, I just thought of something. This way, we'll get a refund on the hospital payments, right? You can keep Valkyrie."

"I'd rather keep you."

"You don't have to choose. Tell the new owner sorry but we're keeping Valkyrie."

"We can talk about this later, okay?"

"Always later with you," she teased, taking the sting away.

The next pain hit but it couldn't dim her happiness even as she panted through it.

Jordan took her hand. "I would take the pain for you if I could."

"That's my cowboy." She grinned at him through her next contraction. "But I'd rather you laid me down and then caught your son."

And at midnight on Christmas Eve James Jordan Hart was born to two parents who loved him as dearly as they loved each other passionately.

* * * * *

A sneaky peek at next month…

Medical Romance™

CAPTIVATING MEDICAL DRAMA—WITH HEART

My wish list for next month's titles…

In stores from 6th December 2013:

❑ From Venice with Love – Alison Roberts

& Christmas with Her Ex – Fiona McArthur

❑ After the Christmas Party… – Janice Lynn

& Her Mistletoe Wish – Lucy Clark

❑ Date with a Surgeon Prince – Meredith Webber

& Once Upon a Christmas Night… – Annie Claydon

Available at WHSmith, Tesco, Asda, Eason, Amazon and Apple

Just can't wait?

Visit us Online

You can buy our books online a month before they hit the shops! **www.millsandboon.co.uk**

1113/03

Special Offers

Every month we put together collections and longer reads written by your favourite authors.

Here are some of next month's highlights— and don't miss our fabulous discount online!

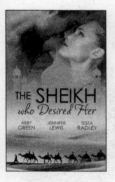

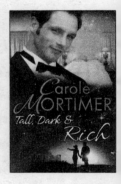

On sale 6th December   **On sale 1st November**   **On sale 6th December**

Work hard, play harder...

Welcome to the Gold Coast, where hearts are broken as quickly as they are healed. Featuring some of the rising stars of the medical world, this new four-book series dives headfirst into Surfer's Paradise.

Available as a bundle at
www.millsandboon.co.uk/medical

Come home this Christmas to Fiona Harper

From the author of *Kiss Me Under the Mistletoe* comes a
Christmas tale of family and fun. Two sisters are ready
to swap their Christmases—the busy super-mum, Juliet,
getting the chance to escape it all on an exotic Christmas
getaway, whilst her glamorous work-obsessed sister,
Gemma, is plunged headfirst into the family Christmas
she always thought she'd hate.

www.millsandboon.co.uk

Wrap up warm this winter with Sarah Morgan…

Sleigh Bells in the Snow

Kayla Green loves business and hates Christmas.

So when Jackson O'Neil invites her to Snow Crystal Resort to discuss their business proposal the last thing she's expecting is to stay for Christmas dinner. As the snowflakes continue to fall, will the woman who doesn't believe in the magic of Christmas finally fall under its spell…?

4th October

www.millsandboon.co.uk/sarahmorgan

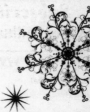

1013/MB435